By
Rocket
to the
Moon

By Rocket to the Moon

The Story of Hans Hardt's
Miraculous Flight

Otto Willi Gail

Illustrated by R. von Crünberg

APOGEE SCIENCE FICTION

By Rocket to the Moon
Originally published 1931
Special contents copyright © 2011
Apogee/Black Cat Press, Burlington, Ontario
Cover illustration by the Rohmer brothers depicting
the take-off of a Max Valier-designed spaceship.

Otto Willi Gail was born July 18,1896, about 150 km north of Munich in Gunzenhausen Germany. He went to school in Augsburg and by the time he was nineteen he found himself serving in the German artillery. During the First World War he watched the impressive growth of the giant German guns and found himself studying the recoil of these huge weapons. Gail had been engrossed by articles in popular magazines about the possibility of spaceflight and he wondered what the implications of recoil would be in a vacuum. Unlike most of his peers, Gail survived the war and soon found himself back at school, continuing his education at the Technical University in Munich. He studied mathematics and physics but in post-war Germany there were few opportunities to make a reasonable living. Gail couldn't afford to keep paying his school fees so he took work selling typewriters and then lumber. He then briefly opened his own business, before closing it down in 1924.

Fortunately, Gail then decided to try his hand at writing fiction. He had been keeping a series of notebooks for several years in which he had been sketching his concepts for spaceships. These drawings would be the basis for his first book about space travel, an imaginative novel called *Der Schuß ins All* (The Shot into Space) which was published in February 1925. The story was also published in a four-page weekly newspaper called *Der Berliner Westen*. The editor of that newspaper decided to send a letter to American rocket pioneer Robert Goddard informing him that they were about to publish Gail's novel. At that time an assortment of German magazines had expressed an interest in the reclusive American inventor's proposed moon rocket. One Berlin newspaper even invited Goddard on a paid lecture tour of Germany, which he politely declined. Goddard thanked them for drawing his attention to Gail's story. Shortly thereafter, in April 1926, Gail sent a copy of his book to Goddard with an enthusiastic letter asking the rocket inventor to read it and possibly help him get it translated and published in America. Three months later Goddard wrote a brief peremptory response in which he implied that he was disinclined to help with the book's translation since it showed the "American contribution" in such a bad light. As the years went by Goddard became less and less cooperative with correspondents working on rockets in Germany. However, Gail was not deterred and since his first novel was such an immediate success he quickly moved on and wrote a sequel in 1926 called *Der Stein vom Mond* (The Stone from the Moon).

On May 19th 1928 his publisher released Gail's *Mit Raketenkraft ins Weltenall* (By Rocketship into the Universe) a non-fiction book partly about his friend Max Valier's experiments with rockets. Just a month later, on June 29th 1928, he followed up this book with a juvenile version of his space stories which appeared under the title *Hans Hardt's Mondfahrt* (Hans Hardt's Trip to the Moon).

In 1929 Gail wrote *Die blaue Kugel* (The Blue Ball) another non-fiction book. Then in the Fall of that year Gail finally realised his ambition to have one of his stories published in English. American publisher Hugo Gernsback had all but invented the science fiction magazine in 1926 when he released the first issue of his *Amazing Stories*. By 1929 Gernsback had been forced into receivership and was compelled to hand over ownership to his creditors. Not to be dissuaded Gernsback immediately formed a new company and launched *Science Wonder Stories*. Gernsback was a European by birth and could read German. He knew that this gave him an advantage over his competitors since this allowed him to choose from the best German and French material for his magazines. In June 1929 Gernsback hired David Lasser as his editor for the new magazine. Lasser would go on to found the *American Interplanetary Society* (today's prestigious AIAA). Lasser and Gernsback decided in the summer of 1929 that they would bring Gail's *The Shot into Space* to American readers. It would appear in the Fall *Science Wonder Stories Quarterly*.

This would be the start of a trend that Gernsback and Lasser would continue for several years. They would publish fiction by members of the *Verein für Raumschiffahrt* (VfR), the *British Interplanetary Society* and the *American Interplanetary Society*. These rocket clubs became fertile breeding grounds for science fiction writers including Gail, Arthur C. Clarke, Philip Cleator, Wernher von Braun, Max Valier, G. Edward Pendray, Nathan Schachner, Laurence Manning, Willy Ley, David Lasser and many others.

By July of 1930 the Journal of the American Rocket Society, *Jet Propulsion*, reported that Gail was a member of the VfR. The highly influential and important German rocket society had been formed in June 1927 by Johannes Winkler, Max Valier and Willy Ley. Gail had clearly been involved with the VfR since its inception and indeed the journal of that group, *Das Rakete*, had run a sample chapter from his first novel in 1927. It had also featured a portrait of Gail alongside such luminaries as Konstantin Tsiolkovsky and Hermann Ganswindt. Other members of the VfR in 1930 included Hermann Oberth, Walter Hohmann (inventor of the Hohmann transfer orbit) Rudolph Nebel, Klaus Riedel, Fritz von Opel (the car manufacturer), Austrian astronautics expert Guido von Pirquet, Russian historian Nikolai Rynin, pioneer theorist Konstantin Tsiolkovsky, Russian space writer Jakow Perlman and French aeronautic pioneer Robert Esnault-Pelterie. Of course most of these were only subscription or honorary members and didn't actually work at the club's famed rocket proving ground. But Valier, Oberth, Opel, Winkler, Ley, Nebel and industrialist Paul Heylandt were all actively involved in rocket research and testing. Gail was almost certainly on hand for many of their early experiments. Later, when Winkler's employer the *Junkers* aircraft company forced him to resign as President of the VfR, he was replaced by Max Valier. Valier was Germany's foremost and most visible publicizer of rocketry and spaceflight and he worked closely with Gail.

During 1930 Gail became a radio celebrity and appeared regularly as a science commentator on *German Hour in Bavaria*. Historian Frank Winter reports that Gail may have used this public position to raise funds for the VfR, presumably while his colleague Valier was still the president of the organisation.

Valier had been impressed by Gail's first book and had corresponded in 1925 about its importance with Hermann Oberth. In April of that year Valier even persuaded a film company in Munich to begin production of a movie of Gail's first novel, with himself acting as technical consultant and playing the character of Engineer Korf, but it was never finished.

Valier would be instrumental in pushing the cause of spaceflight in Germany between 1925 and 1930 and his trust in Otto Willi Gail is evident by the fact that Gail was one of only two people invited to come to the Rüsselsheim test track on April 11th 1928 to witness Valier's latest test run of the Opel *RAK* rocket car prototype. Gail was also witness to the falling-out that transpired between Opel and Valier, which would lead to Valier moving on in search of another sponsor for his rocket experiments.

Max Valier was killed on May 17th 1930 when a liquid fuel rocket exploded on his test bench. Gail wrote of his friend: "He was not concerned with his own gain; if he had been, he would have lost his nerve already a long time ago." Gail would also write Valier's obituary in which he stated, "He sacrificed his last reserves, ran into heavy debts and found himself in personal privation. Anyone else would have given up and looked after his own interests for a change. He had nerves of platinum, if he had any at all."

It may well be Gail's correspondence with David Lasser in America that brought the details about Valier's sad death to the early American rocketeers. Just weeks later Lasser would publish the first ever book to appear in English to take space travel seriously, *The Conquest of Space* which he would dedicate to Valier.

Less than a year later Gail's juvenile novel *Hans Hardt's Mondfahrt* would finally be translated into English and be published by Sears under the title *By Rocket to the Moon*. As intended, it would inspire a generation of young rocket enthusiasts to think about space travel.

INTRODUCTION

CAN it be that Jules Verne's genial conception of a trip to the moon has passed out of the boundless realm of fantasy and stands at the threshold of actual accomplishment?

As a matter of fact, prominent researchers and scientists of many countries are experimenting with and improving a new means of transportation which will whisk us across the seas in a few hours and will, perhaps, carry us far · beyond the boundaries of our Mother Earth: namely, the rocket, whose motive power will be produced by the pressure of gas discharged rearward.

To travel to the moon with our present skyrocket is, of course, impossible, just as it is impossible for a cluster of toy balloons to cross the Atlantic Ocean. From the skyrocket to the spaceship of the future, however, is no farther than from the toy balloon to the transoceanic Zeppelin.

There are two methods of bringing about this development. The first is based on the theory of the German Professor Oberth, of the Association for Cosmic Research in Vienna. He contends that from an ordinary signal rocket, with an improved exhaust construction and operating mechanism, can be evolved a large apparatus capable of traversing the earth's atmospheric mantle into empty space, from which return can be effected by means of parachutes. This space rocket will be provided with automatic measuring and recording instruments. Animals as passengers will first demonstrate the effects of such an extraordinary journey upon rocket occupants. In the event of a successful test, some intrepid soul will be found willing to risk his life as the first rocket passenger for the attractive prospect of being named in history as the Columbus of universal space.

The other solution of this problem has been suggested by Max Valier, aviator and astronomer, of Munich. He proposes to develop the spaceship of the future from the present-day airplane by gradually substituting rearward discharging rockets for the propeller. The intermediate development will be a machine with both propeller and a number of rockets, which will enable a perfectly safe and practicable testing of the rocket device. As the rocket proves itself feasible, exhaust pipes will be more extensively used in subsequent models, until finally the propeller will become superfluous. The result will be a rocket-driven machine, with air-tight cabins, capable of traversing in a few hours the distance from Berlin to New York.

That degree of progress once reached, it will not be a great step from the transoceanic rocket to the spaceship, or the moon rocket.

The great success of my cosmic novels, "The Flight into Eternity" and "The Stone From the Moon", has caused me to use the same material in the form of a boys' adventure story. May Hans Hardt's trip "By Rocket to the Moon" serve to win youth over to the important technical problem involved in a "trip to the universe" and to caution them against the fruitless and often prematurely spoken word "impossible." Even the bicycle has been considered impossible. Will the real Hans Hardt emerge from the ranks of present-day youth?

When a machine succeeds in overcoming a gravitational attraction of about seven and a half miles per second, it will then automatically proceed on a circular course about the earth without further motive power. It will require no wings, because prodigious speed in itself will direct it into a cosmic path of gravity leading into the infinite, as in the case of Professor Oberth's rocket.

It will be some time before such a stage of development is reached. If that point is attained, however, the first rocket-propelled machine will soon follow. Even though that machine be limited to traveling over land, the attempt signifies, nevertheless, the first step in the realization of the age-old dream of the human race—a flight into planetary regions.

And so, the story of Hans Hardt's trip "By Rocket to the Moon" is not merely Utopian. To be sure, Hans Hardt's adventures may appear fantastic. They are, however, a logical consequence of initial accomplishments which can no longer be doubted, and are based on the results of the most recent experimentation in modern natural science.

If this book, besides entertaining the reader, also encourages a spirit of inquiry into the secrets of our sphere, then my fondest hope is realized.

—OTTO WILLI GAIL

I
SEVEN MINUTES PAST TWELVE

TOMMY BIGHEAD'S coupé was proceeding leisurely along the highway toward Detroit. The solitary driver, yawning, leaned back on the soft, leather-upholstered seat of the closed car, holding the wheel carelessly with one hand and looking out sleepily upon the sun-parched country outside. Hotter and hotter the sun beat upon the top of his coupe, making the air inside closer, and Tommy sleepier. Tommy had had a strenuous morning of it.

It was not Tommy's habit to loiter through life at the rate of fifteen miles an hour. On the contrary! The eight cylinders of his motor car were accustomed to full-speed action, and Tommy Bighead was considered the smartest reporter on the *Michigan Evening Post*.

When something interesting happened in the most forsaken corner of the State of Michigan, Tommy Bighead would dash precipitately straight to the spot and ask "What's up?" and would bet that in an hour his story, fresh from the press, would be available at every newsstand in Detroit. He seldom found anyone to take his bet, however, for everyone knew that the alert reporter was not boasting.

There was good reason for him to be squandering his valuable time at the moment. He had just witnessed the launching of a new boat on Lake Erie, and had found occasion to ask "What's up?" so many times that his throat was as dry as tinder and had to be wet at frequent intervals with ice-cold lemonade from a sandwich and soda water stand put up for the occasion by some enterprising concessionaire near the launching dock. But the launching had been uninteresting, and not story enough to make him rush back to his home office.

Softly and monotonously, like a great bee, droned the motor . Tommy was tired, so tired that he was nearly falling asleep; and the car moved more and more slowly, swerving sometimes from: one side to the other of the endless, glittering road ahead of him.

A sharp clatter suddenly aroused Tommy from his drowsiness. His head went up with a start, and was dismayed to find that he was receiving a traveling companion. Outside on the running board stood a tall man, wearing a leather outfit, who was knocking vigorously on the glass.

Tommy quickly came to himself. "The man doesn't look like a thug," he thought. Quick as a flash he shut off the gas and applied the brakes which, shrieking, brought the car to a sudden stop. At the same moment he opened the door.

"What in Heaven's name do you want?" he exclaimed, in a tone that was far from friendly.

The stranger stepped off the running board, bowed shortly but politely, and said in English with a foreign accent: "Pardon the intrusion, sir! I should like to ask you what time it is now?"

"What? That's why you stopped me while I was going full speed?" replied Tommy furiously. Then he muttered something that sounded like "impudence."

"It could hardly be called full speed," calmly answered the stranger. "Anyway, you should be glad that I awakened you before you found yourself reflecting on your carelessness in a roadside grave."

"That's so," said Tommy in embarrassment, and his face became a shade friendlier. "You're right! Thanks! Now, what can I do for you? Speak up! Do you want a lift?"

"No! I am not going to Detroit. I should like to know what time it is now."

"Queer duck!" thought Tommy, reaching for his watch. "It is exactly seven minutes. past twelve."

"Seven minutes past twelve," repeated the stranger. "Thank

you very much. Is your watch reliable?"

"Can you imagine Tommy Bighead without a reliable watch?" retorted Tommy impatiently.

"Very pleased to have met you, Mr. Big—"

"Bighead," supplied Tommy impatiently. "Don't you know the name of the best reporter in Michigan?"

"Are you that?" The man smiled. "Then I can repay your kindness, Mr. Big—Bighead. I have some very interesting news for your paper."

"Good," said Tommy delightedly, and leaned out of the car with a show of interest. "Shoot! What's up? I'll bet that your news is off the press in an hour."

Eagerly he took out his notebook and pencil.

"Write that to-day at noon, at seven minutes past twelve, you spoke with me."

"What else?"

"Nothing else. That is all."

Tommy looked at the stranger suspiciously, as though doubting his soundness of mind, and answered with an aggrieved air: "I will eat my automobile if this news interests a single one of my readers. How much will you bet?"

"I'd be sorry for your nice automobile, Mr. Bighead; because your meeting me is really of great interest for all your readers. You must send out an extra edition immediately!"

"Say, but you have a nerve!" exclaimed the reporter, in exasperation, from his car. "Are you the emperor of Siam or the world's boxing champion!"

"My name is Hans Hardt. I am a German, and I should judge there are not ten men in the United States who know my name," replied the stranger with utter calmness.

Then he drew a parcel from the pocket of his leather coat.

"Here, I have brought you something, Mr. Bighead. It is a bottle of beer, a rare thing in the land of Prohibition, and I hope you will drink the contents to our mutual health."

Tommy was convinced that he was dealing with a lunatic. However, he took the bottle, which was wrapped in a newspaper, and courteously thanked the man for it in order to get rid of him as quickly as possible.

"Another little matter," continued Hans Hardt, as the reporter was about to start the car. "You know that we Germans like to have things in proper form. Would you be good enough to acknowledge in writing the acceptance of the bottle?"

With these words he unfolded and handed a passport through the car window to the surprised reporter; Tommy had no other recourse than to comply with the novel wish of the insistent donor.

"You can send me the bill!" he said rudely, while he scribbled a few words on the passport. "It would not be worth while, sir. Besides, you have forgotten to give the exact time in your receipt. Seven minutes past twelve, please!"

Tommy suppressed an oath, and added the required note.

"Is there anything else I can do for you?"

"No, Mr. Bighead. Thank you!"

"All right. Good-by!"

Tommy sighed with relief as he let the car dash ahead.

"He's nuts," muttered Tommy as, pressing the accelerator to the floor, he speeded on. When he looked back, he no longer saw the stranger, who must have taken to the fields beside the road. Distrustfully he took the bottle from its wrapper.

"Want to see what this queer bird handed me," he said to himself, as he let the porcelain stopper pop up and cautiously sniffed at the opening.

It was indeed real beer, and the German script label proclaimed it to be Muenchener Export beer. Tommy turned the bottle over and over in his hands, then put it back into its newspaper wrapper, wondering what on earth it was all about.

II
THE BOTTLE OF BEER

HALF an hour later Tommy entered the editorial room of the *Michigan Evening Post*.

"Hello, Tommy!" greeted the editor-in-chief. "Have you heard the latest?"

"Naturally, Mr. Tiller!"

"No, Tommy. You haven't heard it. You couldn't. have heard it. Or have you been in Germany this morning?"

The reporter became suddenly attentive.

"In Germany? No. But a German..." He interrupted himself. "Go on, old man. What were you going to tell me?"

"A wireless message just came over from Berlin by way of New York."

"That's nothing new," said Tommy, sarcastically. "Hardly a week goes by that a non-stop flight from Berlin to New York is not announced with great hullabaloo. Nice little sporting adventures, like the trip of Captain Koehl from Ireland to Labrador, for instance, do not satisfy."

"Yes," replied Tiller. "That's why I wish this Hans Hardt's flight would succeed."

Tiller stopped speaking; he had to, for Tommy Bighead, the smartest reporter in Michigan, had jumped up like a shot out of a gun, and had grabbed his chief by the neck.

"Tommy!" gasped Tiller in terrified amazement. The reporter let go, then in mad frenzy began to perform a grotesque Indian dance in the editorial room, overturning chairs, sweeping down rows of books from the desk, and making such a racket that the windows fairly rattled.

"Lunatic! clumsy idiot!" and other similarly complimentary expressions were flying about.

In consternation, the chief watched Tommy's wild antics.

"In Heaven's name, Tommy, have you had a sunstroke, or have you eaten something that has sent you dotty?"

Abruptly Tommy stopped. He made a few more futile passes into space, then he pulled up a chair, sat down on it, replaced the end of his cigar in the corner of his mouth, and said with an air of regained composure: "Brought you an article on the flight of Hans Hardt."

"It is already in the composing room."

"Well, add more to it—no! Put out an extra edition: Hans Hardt lands in America! The German trans-Atlantic flight successfully completed."

"Tommy," replied Tiller solicitously, "Tommy, I'm worried about you. Do you want to take a vacation?"

"Don't talk nonsense, old man. What would happen to the Michigan Evening Post if Tommy Bighead went on a vacation?"

"Allowing for your keenness, Tommy, how do you know that the flier has landed? Did you dream about him?"

"No," replied Tommy drily. "Spoke to him—an hour ago!"

The chief burst out laughing.

"Tommy!" he said. "You are seeing ghosts, and you absolutely must take a vacation. Do you know what time the flight started?"

"No."

"At four-thirty..."

"What? Yesterday afternoon at four-thirty?

Then he flew mighty fast."

Tiller held his sides from laughter.

"No, Tommy! Not yesterday! To-day! At four-thirty this afternoon he started—to-day!"

"Go chase yourself!" Tommy angrily grated through his teeth. "It's scarcely one o'clock now!"

"According to our time, Tommy! But the report comes from

Germany, and Central European time is six hours ahead of ours! Let's figure it out. Four-thirty less six—that makes ten-thirty. Correct?"

Tommy turned uneasily in his chair.

"Then according to our time the start was made at ten-thirty this morning. That's absolutely impossible!"

"How so?"

"Because I spoke with Hans Hardt shortly after twelve o'clock," obstinately persisted Tommy.

"You've been seeing things, Tommy! You've had too many cold drinks, haven't you? Or do you really believe that a man can fly like a flash of lightning across the Atlantic in an hour and a half, no more than time for lunch."

"No."

Tommy sat for a time silent and motionless.

Tiller saw that he was deep in thought.

"What's eating you, Tommy... "

"I guess Tommy Bighead is a fit subject for the insane asylum, Mr. Tiller," answered the reporter somberly, gazing at the ash end of his cigar as though seeking there the solution of the puzzle.

Tiller nodded with apparent unconcern and racked his brains for a consoling reply.

Suddenly Tommy's face lighted up with joy. "Jumping Jupiter—the bottle!" he shouted, and he sprang out into the hall, dashed down the elevator to the parked car in the street, seized Hans Hardt's gift, knocked over a boy in his path and rushed back to Tiller.

"Tiller," he cried out before reaching the door, "since when have ghosts been giving away bottles of beer? Here, taste it! Real Muenchner Export beer! It's a little warm."

"Did your Hans Hardt give you this?" Tiller shook his head incredulously.

"Sure thing! At seven minutes past twelve sharp—on the road twenty miles south of Detroit! Shall we bet?"

Tiller now became thoughtful, because when Tommy proposed a bet there was something back of it.

"Well," he said, "that was a generous ghost, anyhow! But how can you explain the whole story, Tommy?"

"Have you ever heard the story of the hare and the tortoise, Mr. Tiller?"

"Hare and tortoise? How...?"

"The two...?"

"Certainly there are two! The one Hans Hardt in Europe pretends to fly across the Atlantic Ocean. The other hangs around here and favors me with this neat present. To prove his alibi, he had the receipt written in his passport. Do you see through the swindle?"

Tommy looked triumphantly at his chief. He was obviously proud of his shrewdness, and in the best of humors he unfolded the wrapper from the bottle. Suddenly his eyes became fixed. He fell back in his chair as though about to faint, and his arms hung lifelessly downwards.

"Tommy!"

Tiller anxiously approached the reporter. "Read," answered Tommy in a colorless voice. The editor-in-chief seized the paper in which the bottle had been wrapped, and paled as he read: *Muenchner Latest News.* Evening Edition of July 17."

Without a word he looked at Tommy and pointed with a dull smile to the calendar on the wall.

"Good Lord!" uttered Tommy, overcome.

"A German paper—brought over from Germany—to-day!" he groaned. "In fact, brought over in an hour and a half!"

Perfect silence ensued for a time in the editorial room of the Michigan Evening Post. Only the typewriters rattled in the next room.

III
THE HOLE IN THE SKY

TOMMY'S head was clear now. The eight cylinders of his car no longer droned sleepily, but whirred and sputtered furiously, and with fifty-horse-power impetus the long car raced through Detroit's wilderness of houses. He paid no attention to the imprecations of pedestrians and automobile drivers, but with firm grip on the wheel kept his attention fixed on the traffic-crowded street ahead.

The last dingy, barn-like houses of the south quarter flew past, followed by manufacturing plants, deserted camp sites, and fields. The road was clear. Tommy stepped harder on the gas. The speedometer needle moved forward over the scale, paused at seventy-five miles, crept ahead. The trees bordering the road were no longer distinguishable; they were blurred into a solid mass like the edge of a woods.

Fred Tiller, the editor-in-chief, sat beside Tommy. Cautiously he touched his arm.

"Don't be reckless, Tommy. Eighty-five miles an hour will land us in a coffin!"

Tommy laughed shortly. "What time is it?" he asked.

"One twenty-five."

"O.K."

And the mad ride continued. Five minutes passed in this manner. Tiller heaved a sigh of relief when the impetuous driver finally shut off the gas and stopped, looking searchingly around.

"This must be the spot where Hans Hardt held me up an hour and a half ago."

"What direction did he take afterwards?"

"1 don't know," replied Tommy sullenly. "My brain wasn't tracking. Must look around."

Tommy drove ahead very slowly, and both men watched the sides of the road.

"There's a path branching off to the right, Tommy. Perhaps...?"

"Maybe. Let's try it."

The car swerved sharply to the right and proceeded with difficulty along a worn, rutted road. Tommy cursed volubly at the holes and stones which impeded their progress and caused them to slow down. On a slight up-grade the road led through wheatfields and wound around a clump of sloebushes higher up.

"Hold it!" shouted Tommy and jammed on the brakes. He was about to collide with a huge, heavily-laden truck which was coming from behind the bushes, and, grinding like a steam-roller, was rumbling on toward the smart little coupe.

The road was so narrow that it was impossible for the two cars to pass each other, and the only way out was for Tommy to reverse and back downhill.

"What is that fool doing on this terrible road?" queried Tiller.

Tommy, whose attention was on the road behind while backing down, had no time to consider the question.

"Maybe we can back into the field this way." He had misjudged, however, the depth of the overgrown ditch which separated the road from the field. With a jolt the left back wheel sank into the ditch, the right spun futilely around in the air, and the car would not budge from the spot.

"Nice mess!" grumbled the reporter angrily, while he threw open the door and jumped out.

The truck lumbered ahead to within three yards, but could not get by.

"Hi, there!" called out Tommy to the driver. "Have you a jack?"

The driver nodded with a grin and climbed slowly down from his high seat.

"Listen, Tommy, do you hear anything?" Tommy had already

started. In long strides he ran up the slope, and Tiller followed him, panting. The four men working on the car paused and looked toward the west.

Sharp reports, like a gun salute, sounded over the field. Then, silence.

"Hold on, Tommy," called Tiller after the swift-moving reporter.

"No time," Tommy called back. "Over there back of the slope is Hans Hardt...and..."

The reports sounded again, more loudly than before, and changed quickly into a hissing roar. "Look!" cried Tommy, and he stopped, breathing heavily.

About eight hundred yards to the west a gigantic flying machine rose into the air, its wings gleaming in the sun.

"Too late!" groaned Tommy in chagrin, and with open mouth he watched the machine rising almost perpendicularly toward the east and leaving behind a white trail. It became perceptibly smaller, and presently the details were lost to sight.

"Unusual type," said Tiller, who had in the meantime caught up with his companion.

"You're right. A huge body on disproportionately small wings."

"Where do you come from with your truck? What's up?"

The driver merely pointed his thumb over his shoulder and said nothing.

"What kind of barrels are those on your load?" continued Tommy. The man shrugged his shoulders and made no reply. Nothing could be gotten out of him, and three other men crouched on the load maintained a sphinx-like silence.

Tommy's main concern was to get his car started. The truck driver with his' three comrades brought over a large jack to lift the car out of the ditch.

Tommy took advantage of the situation to look more closely at the load on the truck. He ran his finger lightly around the open bunghole in one of the apparently empty barrels and cautiously licked it with his tongue.

• Otto Willi Gail

"Oho!" he said, smiling, and gave a soft whistle. Cautiously he beckoned to Tiller.

"Do you want to earn a reward, Mr. Tiller?" he said in an undertone. "Report these people to the Prohibition officers. Wholesale bootleggers."

"Humph! Empty barrels don't prove a thing, Tommy," replied Tiller, grinning. Suddenly he stopped, motionless.

"Did you ever before hear a propeller whistle so queerly, Tommy?"

"No. A noise like a steamship siren is not caused by a propeller, Tiller, and no gasoline motor leaves such a heavy trail of smoke behind. A mighty queer machine!"

The mysterious flying machine was by this time a little black speck in the blue sky, and both men craned their necks to follow its flight.

"I simply can't figure out," said Tiller reflectively, "how this contraption can cover a stretch of six thousand miles in an hour and a half. It doesn't fly much faster than our commercial airplanes."

"Look!" cried Tommy excitedly. "Do you see the flashes?"

"Thundering blazes! What's that? The thing is exploding. Why in Heaven's name didn't we bring a field glass!"

In the wake of the machine appeared a streak of fire accompanied by a thick cloud of smoke. For a few seconds came the sound of distant explosions which immediately died out.

The flying machine had disappeared, leaving only a thin trail of smoke against the cloudless sky, which tapered out and vanished in the wind.

The men stood for a time in speechless consternation. Finally Tiller said in a hesitating voice: "It's a shame, Tommy. Hans Hardt's a goner."

"No, I don't believe it!" answered Tommy drily.

"But after those explosions the machine vanished without leaving a trace. Or can you see it yet?"

"No, I see nothing but smoke."

"Where could it have gone, then, Tommy?"

"Perhaps it slipped through a hole in the sky, Tiller."

Upon an angry silence on the part of the chief, Tommy said in a conciliatory tone: "You shouldn't fly up like that, Mr. Tiller. I didn't intend to hurt your feelings. Do you think that a machine which travels six thousand miles in an hour and a half could behave like an ordinary machine? I think the take-off we saw was only a preliminary to the actual traveling which began with that queer explosion. Well, I'll bel can't make it out. Maybe it opened a hole in the sky where it has slipped through. These Germans are wizards. You never know what they're up to!"

Tiller, during Tommy's unusually long speech, had been watching the truck. The four men had hoisted the coupe from the ditch and pushed it back so that the truck could pass by.

"Tommy," said Tiller, "those people are going off without waiting for us to thank them."

"No matter, Mr. Tiller. I have taken the number of the truck-F200I. I'm positive those tight-mouthed bootleggers are in some way connected with Hans Hardt. I'll make them talk. Want to bet?"

IV
F200I

ON the way back the chief wrote the copy for the headlines to be inserted in the evening edition. He got out at the Post building to leave the copy in the composing room.

In the meantime Tommy dashed to the nearest telephone booth.

"Hello! Hello! Is this the Automobile Registration Bureau? Hello! This is Tommy Bighead—O.K—of the *Evening Post*. Will you please look up the name of the owner of the twenty-fIve-ton truck, license number F00I? Yes."

In less than a minute came the information: "F200I is owned by Longfields Brothers in the Eighth District."

"Good. Thanks."

Tommy looked up the number of the firm in the telephone book and made the call.

"Longfields Brothers," promptly answered a Woman's voice.

"Hello. I need immediately a heavy truck—at least twenty-five tons."

"I'm sorry, our twenty-five-ton truck is in use. Could you use two smaller ones?"

"That won't do. I must have the big one."

"It has been rented for three days."

"Perhaps I can make an arrangement with the one who is renting it. What's his name?"

"Mr. Hardt."

Tommy nodded in satisfaction and said in the tone of one who has heard good news:

"Oh, Mr. Hardt. That's luck. He's an old friend of mine. He is staying at the Metropolis Hotel, isn't he?"

"No, he's at MacAllan's Hotel on Boston Street."

Tommy then added: "I tried to see him a while ago, but he had left for Europe."

"Left? That can't be. Mr. Hardt was here in our office two minutes ago."

Tommy almost dropped the receiver with surprise and forgot to answer. "Well, if that isn't—" he said to himself. "Hardt here yet?"

Stunned, he sat for a few moments, trying vainly to collect his thoughts. "Have we been hoodwinked," he muttered ill-humoredly, as he finally arose.

Then he drove to Boston Street, stopped at MacAllan's Hotel, and entered the hall.

"Yes, sir," the clerk replied courteously to his question. "Mr. Hardt has Room 45"—looking for the key—"and he seems to be in, because the key for Number 45 isn't here."

Tommy took out a visiting card and had himself announced.

A moment later a light appeared on the telephone switchboard.

"Mr. Hardt is awaiting you in the smoking room on the eighth floor," reported a bellhop.

Tommy, following him, stepped into the elevator and rode in tense expectation to the eigth floor.

V
THE MYSTERY OF
HANS HARDT

MR. Tommy Bighead," announced the boy and disappeared.

Tommy stood in the presence of short, slight, unassuming gentleman whose age was a matter of conjecture. His well-kept little grey beard and thin, closely wrinkled face formed a striking contrast with his animated eyes which, sparkling with youthful vivacity through horn-rimmed glasses, compelled one's attention.

"I beg your pardon, sir," said Tommy more politely than was his custom. "There must be mistake. I wanted to see Mr. Hardt."

"I am her. What can I do for you?"

Tommy scrutinized the face of the grey-haired man, shook his head and said: "Do you know me, sir?"

"You are Mr. Tommy Bighead from the Michigan Evening Post," answered the other, smiling. "You sent me your card."

"True! But you have seen me once before, sIr?"

"I have only just had the honor of making your acquaintance."

"Then you can't be the Mr. Hans Hardt I'm looking for."

"I am certainly not the one. My name is Alexander Hardt— Doctor Alexander Hardt—I am a German archeologist, and I intend to go to New York to-night in order to make the fast boat to Hamburg. Does that suit you, Mr. Bighead?"

"Oh," said Tommy thoughtfully, shifting from one foot to the other. He hesitated a moment before asking the all important question: "Do you know your namesake, Hans Hardt, Professor?"

With throbbing pulse, Tommy waited in feverish anxiety for

the reply. He was resigned to encountering new difficulties in hearing an indifferent negative reply; though he was by no means willing to let himself be put off the scent with subterfuges. He had prepared plenty of questions to get the truth out of this German.

Great was Tommy's surprise when Dr. Hardt calmly answered: "Yes, Hans Hardt is my nephew. If you want to talk with him, you are too late. He was here-in the city-this morning, but"—looking at his wristwatch—"soon now he will be in Germany. Won't you be seated, Mr. Bighead?"

Tommy sat down in the easy chair proffered him, and looked helplessly around. To discover thus near at hand the key to the mystery which he was attempting to unravel was the one possibility on which he had not counted, and now that he was on the threshold of a solution of the puzzle, the unbelievable happened! Tommy Bighead, the smartest reporter in the State of Michigan, did not know what question to ask first.

"M-M-M-Mr. Hardt," stammered Tommy, "if y-y-you had t-t-told this to s-s-somebody else, he would have telephoned for an alienist."

"It is a consolation to me, Mr. Bighead, that you have a more flattering opinion of me. Do you want to ask anything more?"

Tommy experienced an inexplicable shyness before this small, shrunken man, and for some reason he felt oppressed under the searching gaze of the scientist's keen eyes.

"Hans Hardt, then, has really flown from Germany to the United States in an hour and a half?" he inquired, still doubting.

"Yes, from Friedrichshafen on Lake Constance to Detroit it took him exactly ninety minutes."

Excitedly the reporter went on with his questions: "How is it possible that an East to West hop was accomplished in such an unbelievably short time? Is Hans Hardt omnipotent that he can control the storms on the sea that arise from the West?"

"Certainly not! But he has traveled over a route which is free from storms."

"I can't exactly imagine where one is to find such a route.

Dr. Hardt thoughtfully tapped his fingertips together.

"Well, at an altitude of more than forty-five thousand feet, for instance, Mr. Bighead, every perceptible air current stops."

"What do you say!" burst from Tommy.

"Then he has also broken the former altitude record!"

The scientist smiled.

"Yet, at an altitude of nine miles it would be impossible to travel six thousand miles in an hour and a half. No machine in the world could overcome the resistance of the air, which, at such a speed would be prodigious. No, Hans Hardt had to go much higher! I should judge that for a stretch he flew five hundred miles above the rainbow."

The reporter presented a picture of total perplexity.

"But, Dr. Hardt," he cried, "you're raving. At that altitude there is no more air, and—if there is..."

"You are quite right, Mr. Bighead. The trajectory of flight ran for the most part in the non-resisting void outside of the atmospheric belt around the earth. And that is the whole secret of this unprecedented speed in traveling."

For a time there was perfect silence in the room. Tommy gulped as though he had swallowed the wrong way

"I must confess, sir," he then said, "that I am beginning to doubt my own sanity. It is quite clear to me that greater speed is possible in a void than in atmosphere which opposes resistance to all motion. But how can a flying machine stay up in a void? The whole theory of flying, according to my knowledge, is based on the fact that wings are supported by air. I will drink Lake Erie dry if any flying machine does not instantly break up on entering the void."

Tommy Bighead had spoken positively in his eagerness. Dr. Hardt made no answer. He arose, took a tightly stuffed pillow from the divan, and went to the extreme end of the smoking room.

"Look out! Catch it! There you are!"

And in a high curve he threw the pillow in Tommy's direction.

The reporter was not quick enough, however, and the pillow landed on his head.

"I beg your pardon," he growled. "What are you trying to prove?"

"I am demonstrating to you, Mr. Bighead, how an object can fly without wings," replied the scientist, resuming his seat opposite Tommy. "Do you believe that this pillow required the air in the room to travel the distance from my hand to your—excuse me—head, where it landed?"

"No," said Tommy in surprise. Hardt laughed.

"Then take back immediately your promise to drink Lake Erie dry. The disadvantage might be yours."

"The deuce," muttered the reporter, while he tugged at his collar as though it were choking him. "I'm tumbling. Hans Hardt did not exactly fly over the ocean, but was shot over to us in a high curve from Germany."

He looked impatiently at the German, and, as the latter nodded an affirmative, he jumped up.

"Then bet with me, sir," he cried, and his reporter's effrontery again came into evidence. "If I tell my readers in to-morrow morning's edition that a human being has been shot over here from a big gun, I'll be lynched and be a dead man by noon."

"You should not tell your readers such unplausible tales, Mr. Bighead!"

Tommy Bighead became tense.

"So, you've been making a fool of me. Darned if I can't play at that game, too."

"How is that? You must admit that the huge gun is your own invention. Did I say anything about a huge gun?"

"No," curtly replied Tommy. "Probably it was a bird-shot gun."

Dr. Hardt deliberated for a moment. Finally, in a tone sharply contrasting with his previous mildness, he said: "Will you cease your little pleasantries, Mr. Bighead, or shall we terminate this interview?"

Tommy hastened to reply in an apologetic tone. "I'm sorry, Dr. Hardt. But what you've been saying is beyond me."

"Not at all, if you would take the trouble to think about it. Had my nephew been shot upward by a great cannon, he most certainly would have been blown to pieces by the violence of the circulation of your paper will doubtless be doubled when your article on Hans Hardt appears."

"It's a pity you won't tell me what alcohol has to do with all this. That's the thing that would go big in America. I'm only afraid nobody will believe the story, and then where will Tommy Bighead's reputation be?"

"They will have to believe it. You have incontestable proof. Did you notice the newspaper wrapped around the bottle?"

"That's so. To-day's paper from Germany proves something. You're right. Nobody can question the evidence."

"I am glad you noticed the newspaper. My nephew could not very well call your attention to it at the time. If he had done so, you would have followed him, and he wanted especially to avoid that. Nobody, except a few of the initiated, was permitted to see the machine."

Tommy failed to mention that he had seen it, though his glimpse had been but a fleeting one.

"How was it, then," he queried in open wonderment, "that such an undertaking was kept quiet?"

"That is simple. Everybody who knew about it kept quiet."

"Then how do you happen to be telling me about it? Don't forget you haven't made me promise to keep quiet."

"You may say or write as much as you see fit. Now that the first attempt has been successful and my nephew's machine has left this country, there is no longer any necessity of withholding the facts regarding it. Quite the contrary. We now want the public to know all about it, for we need capital to construct a larger machine. The enterprise which my nephew has next in view will require thousands of dollars, and the private means heretofore at our disposal are nearly exhausted."

Galvanized by a sudden inspiration, Tommy leaned eagerly forward.

"You need money, Mr. Hardt?" The scientist nodded.

"How much?"

"At least fifty thousand dollars."

"Good! I'll see that you get two hundred and fifty thousand dollars," said Tommy, without hesitation.

"From what source?"

"From the trust to which the *Michigan Evening Post* belongs."

"We would not want to consider assistance of that kind," replied Dr. Hardt somewhat coldly. "My nephew's work has been and will continue to be a private enterprise."

"That's all right," agreed Tommy in some amusement. "The money will be given to you, you may do with it whatever you like, and you will be held accountable for it to no one."

"But there must be some condition. Nobody gives away two hundred and fifty thousand dollars for nothing."

"Of course not, Mr. Hardt. However, my condition won't be much of an obstacle to you."

"And that is?" asked the Doctor, obviously interested.

"That you continue to keep your project a secret, and refuse to give any information to or to be interviewed by the newspapers. You must cable your nephew immediately to say nothing until you have seen him. Let's hope in the meantime that not too much has leaked out to the public."

"Is this assurance the only thing you want in exchange for such a large sum?"

"No. Another little condition has to be included," said Tommy, with a smile of satisfaction. "Your nephew will continue his work in secrecy. In spite of that, every newspaper will write about him and about what he is doing. And where will the newspapers get their information? From Hans Hardt's only authorized representative—Tommy Bighead. And he," added Tommy triumphantly, "will set the price so high that he will make a nice little profit on the investment. That's the proposition."

Hardt hesitated.

"Your proposal is worth considering, Mr. Bighead," he said thoughtfully. "I cannot, however, make any decision without my nephew's approval."

"Well, why don't you postpone your trip till to-morrow and send your nephew a cable. I'll put it through as a press cablegram, which will go much quicker. We could have an answer in five hours. In the meantime, I'll talk with my chief, Mr. Tiller, and get his O.K. on the amount. Then if Hans Hardt agrees, we will start together for Germany to-morrow. Is it a go?"

Dr. Hardt's expression betrayed astonishment at the dispatch with which this brisk young American settled matters. In any event, the proposition seemed advantageous and he accepted it.

"One thing more, Dr. Hardt," said Tommy, as he arose to take leave. "Won't you tell me in advance what the next venture is to be? Is it, by any chance, a non-stop flight to Australia?"

"Farther, much farther than that!"

"Oh, I get you!" exclaimed Tommy quickly.

"He will make a non-stop trip around the world. That will be a wonderful accomplishment."

Hardt shook his head, smiling mysteriously.

"Farther! Much farther!" he slowly repeated.

"Farther still?" stammered Tommy, nonplused. "It's impossible to go farther than that."

"Nevertheless..."

The German went up to the reporter and, looking him steadily in the eye, said: "You are the first outsider to learn of it, Mr. Bighead. This hop across the Atlantic was nothing but a test flight, a mere tryout, like the feeble grasshopper jumps with which the Wright brothers inaugurated flying thirty years ago."

"And your ultimate destination?" asked Tommy eagerly.

"Is a journey to—the Universe. Hans Hardt will be the first man to leave this planet."

Slowly and emphatically Dr. Hardt made this arresting statement, and his eyes beamed with pride in his extraordinary nephew.

"Good heavens!" And Tommy Bighead collapsed in silence.

VI
ANDERL

I T was still early afternoon as Tommy Bighead, bursting with news, drove back to his office. Simultaneously, on the other side of the Atlantic Ocean, gray dusk was creeping from mountain and valley over the wide, shimmering surface of Lake Constance. The lofty peaks toward the south were aglow in the rays of the setting sun, whose ruddy reflection imperceptibly shifted from the shadowy depths to the leaden-colored sky. The radiant evening star, Venus, was beginning to sparkle above the woody slopes bordering the west shore of the lake. The wind, which had ruffled the great expanse of water in the afternoon, was now still, and the last receding waves gently plashed against the shore.

All was quiet in the great aviation construction plant to the north of Friedrichshafen. Only on the landing float were a few workers setting up huge searchlights for the night.

Far out on the lake, scarcely visible from the shore, rested a small motorboat, a mere dark speck on the water. The engine was shut off, and the retreating waves rippled noiselessly against the sides of the small craft. The pilot at the helm glanced at the clock on the switchboard, saying in a preoccupied tone, "Something must have happened to him; it is almost nine o'clock."

"Don't give up so soon," replied the other occupant of the boat, whose name was Anderl.

"Keep your ears open."

Anderl was an uncouth Bavarian lad who had been employed at the construction plant as a mechanic three years before. At first he had entirely escaped notice, for he was only a mechanic, Andreas Lindpointner. As time went on, however, he became a subject of remark. One of the reasons was his persistent refusal to exchange his native costume for the customary blue outfit of the mechanics. The leather breeches which he wore year after year were as though he had grown into them. Furthermore, he found it difficult to adopt a language very different from his native dialect. He still retained the crude, informal mode of expression, characteristic of the Bavarian vernacular, and used the familiar second person pronoun on occasions requiring the more formal third person. These peculiarities doubtless would have led him into difficulties, had not his fellow-workers, won by his rough but kindly good humor, been of a disposition to understand and tolerate his eccentricity of speech and dress.

One day Hans Hardt, chief engineer of the construction plant, had given him a particularly difficult problem in construction to carry out. He had accepted the task with enthusiasm, exclaiming, "I'll do that, Mr. Hardt. You can depend upon Anderl!" From that time on, Andreas Lindpointner was known only as "Anderl."

Hardt became increasingly aware that the sincere, spontaneous country lad had more real ability than many of the engineers. He took occasion to try out Anderl in his private experimental workshop. In this manner he found that Anderl not only could handle tools with some skill, but also could hold his tongue. And so, in the course of time, Anderl became Hans Hardt's confidential helper.

At length there came a red-letter day for Anderl. From some unknown cause an explosion occurred in the experimental workshop, and in the space of a few seconds the entire building was in flames. Anderl and his two companions were able to reach safety, but Hans Hardt was missing.

Anderl rushed frantically back into the seething flames, shouting, "Hardt is still in the battery room!" With head lowered, he drove his massive shoulders against a door, which burst open with a shower of splinters.

Stifled by the smoke and by the gas from the storage batteries,

Hans Hardt lay unconscious on the floor.

Anderl slung the heavy body of the big man like a sack over his shoulders, and bore him over burning rafters and through crumbling walls into the open. With his own, as well as Hans Hardt's, clothes aflame and no time to lose, he dashed to the edge of the lake and let himself and his burden into the water.

For days Hardt hovered between life and death. Anderl, too, was seriously burned. He merely had his wounds dressed, however, and refused to budge from the bedside of his chief. When Hardt finally regained consciousness and learned who had been his rescuer, he clasped Anderl's clumsy fist in his two hands, saying, "I shall not forget this, Anderl." The huge uncouth youth wept like a child, so happy was he at these friendly words of his master.

From then on, Anderl became Hardt's shadow.

He was indispensable as helper, mechanic, personal attendant, confidential advisor and trusted friend—all in one. Master and helper worked together, with single purpose, and Anderl was the only person in the world who was aware of Hardt's prodigious plans for the future down to the minutest detail.

VII
THE OCEAN HOP
COMPLETED

THE two men listened in the darkness. They heard the sound of a steamer heaving through the waves; a motorboat horn shrilled now and then; and from the shore came the snort and rumble of a train.

Anderl nudged his companion. "Do you hear anything?"

The other shook his head.

"It seemed as though—there it is again!" From afar sounded a deep, scarcely audible

rumble, as of an invisible storm approaching from behind the mountains. The rumble lasted only three seconds and then died out.

"I know that voice," said Anderl, his broad face lighting with a grin. "It's he. He has entered the air circle, or we could not tell the direction from which the sound came. He'll be here directly."

Four minutes elapsed. There was no further rumble to be heard.

"You're wrong, Anderl," dubiously commented the mechanic.

"The dickens I am! Look up there!"

Away up in the sky a dim point of light appeared, disappeared, reappeared at regular intervals.

"Those are Morse signals. Do you suppose any little angel in Heaven could flash the Morse code like that? It is Hardt, as sure as I am Anderl. Let her loose now, so that we won't be late."

The motor started up and the bow of the boat cut through the churning water.

On shore the searchlights blazed forth, their rays groping through the dark like giant fingers to illuminate the path of the flying machine when it came within range of their light.

Anderl's boat was hovering near the landing float.

"It will be a little while yet before he can come down," called the engineer who was operating the searchlights.

Anderl nodded. "Yes, he has far too much speed to land."

The speck in the sky curved in wide circles above the lake. With every curve it came lower, then inclined toward the north and disappeared momentarily from view.

"He must first lose his speed through the retarding influence of the air resistance," commented Anderl, with the authority of an expert.

When the machine finally reappeared, it was gliding only 600 feet above the lake. With a loud roar it swooped down in a spiral curve. The impact of the pontoons against the surface of the water sent up a high fountain of spray. Its speed rapidly decreased through contact with the water until finally the powerful machine came to a stop in front of the landing float. Like a gigantic, ghostly bird, it gleamed with metallic luster in the blinding glare of the searchlights.

Anderl's boat was the first to reach the side of the weird, propellerless monster. Its wings, veined with exhaust pipes which had their outlet toward the rear, extended out like a great flat roof.

Anderl climbed nimbly up a ladder to the smooth body, and looked through a port window into the interior of the air-tight cabin. There in the electric illumination, scarcely recognizable in the thick leather helmet which concealed his head, sat Hans Hardt. Anderl, who was familiar with every detail of the machine's construction, turned a valve cap and thus released the air from the cabin until the pressure inside was equal to that outside. Immediately afterwards, a small door was opened from the interior.

"Welcome home, Mr. Hardt," cried Anderl, joyfully waving his green cap.

"Hello, there, Anderl," came the hearty reply.

"Has everything gone all right, Mr. Hardt?"

"Yes, Anderl, everything has gone well."

Anderl gave a glad shout, which ended the conversation.

A motor tug towed the machine to the shore, where it was

anchored with a strong chaip.. Hans Hardt stepped onto the landing float. The ocean hop had been successfully completed.

It was only a small group that welcomed the flier on his return. Although it had become generally known that Hans Hardt had started the flight to America, nobody but the few intimately connected with his project could conceive of his returning on the same day that he had started. Moreover, as the arrival of a large flying machine at the field was an every-day occurrence, there were no outside spectators.

Thus ended, as it had begun, Hans Hardt's trans-Atlantic flight, quietly, unobtrusively, and without publicity of any sort. The lack of noise and confusion was a relief to the weary flier after the strain of his eventful day. He briefly greeted the engineers and rode home with the business manager of the construction plant, Mr. Kamphenkel. Anderl, sitting next to the chauffeur, was as proud as though he himself had flown to America.

"Have you actually been in America to-day?" queried Kamphenkel, to reassure himself that the stupendous event was a reality.

"Positively. At exactly seven minutes past twelve by American time I gave a bottle of beer to a journalist over there. The poor man was mystified by my behavior."

Kamphenkel seized the engineer's hand and exclaimed with fervor: "Forgive me for doubting your achievement. An old man like myself doesn't grasp new things so easily. You have effectively demonstrated that a rocket driven by a liquid fuel can produce the result upon which you calculated, and I no longer doubt your success in overcoming the resistance of the air. It is almost beyond comprehension. The mere thought that a human being can entirely leave the earth is most upsetting."

"My first trip, however, did not proceed entirely according to program, Mr. Kamphenkel," replied Hardt seriously. "For a while everything went all right. I ascended, as in an ordinary airplane, to an altitude of 13,000 feet. Then I started the first projection. For exactly two minutes I let the exhaust pipes work full force. With the pressure thus obtained from the backward explosions, my speed was increasing at the rate of 100 feet a second, and at the expiration of the two minutes I had reached a speed of two and a quarter miles a second. Then, with fuel shut off, my machine shot ahead under this projectile force. In half an hour I was penetrating the final air strata and had covered about 3,000 miles. In the second projection the exhaust pipes were performing to scarcely more than half their capacity, the projectile force was correspondingly weaker, and I had to turn on the fuel for the third time in order to reach America."

"How do you account for this decreased effectiveness in operation?"

"Probably the reason lies in the sudden cooling off of the exhaust pipes during the free trip through airless space. I was, for the most part, high above the air circle in the space beyond the earth which has no heat. In the future construction of such machines some means must be devised to heat the exhaust pipes before starting their operation."

"In the space beyond the earth," said Kamphenkel musingly. "Please go on. How was the landing?"

"Oh, that was accomplished smoothly. I descended gradually so that the air worked like a brake, without, however, opposing sufficient resistance to heat my apparatus. In this manner my speed was checked by more than 300 feet a second, and I could glide down as in an ordinary airplane. The small, isolated lake south of Detroit, which Dr. Hardt selected, proved a practicable landing and taking-off place. Through being obliged to make the three projections, however, instead of the two upon which I had counted, my fuel was nearly exhausted. I should be over there yet if it had not been for my uncle, who remained in Detroit purposely to provide additional fuel. It might not have been so easy for me to secure large quantities of alcohol in a country under Prohibition."

The engineer became silent. "And the return trip?"

"I had a little trouble then, too. The American alcohol must have been adulterated, and its heating power was considerably reduced. I therefore needed great acceleration power so as to reach as quickly as possible the necessary projecting speed. And then,"

Hardt smiled wryly, "the pressure became too strong for me. I scarcely had the strength to shut off the exhaust pipes for the free trip. I must have been unconscious for a time. During the swift passage over the projectile curve it did not matter, but if I hadn't returned to consciousness before my machine shot into the air, it would have burned without a doubt."

"Great heavens!" exclaimed Kamphenkel in alarm. "It was a monstrous risk for you to take this first trip alone. But you wouldn't be stopped."

"There was no other way, Mr. Kamphenkel. As you know, our means were not sufficient to construct an apparatus large enough to hold two persons. People want to see results before they put their money into a scheme like this."

"Well, it won't be so easy, in spite of your marvelous results," commented the business manager, "to raise money in this impoverished Germany of ours for something which doesn't promise immediate returns."

"That is quite true," agreed Hardt, little pleased by the thought. "There will be no money gained, either, by my contemplated trip to the moon."

The car drew up to the entrance of Hardt's home. Anderl hastened to open the door. "Anderl," said Hardt, as he stepped out, "if we had enough money, you and I would travel together next time."

Anderl grinned, showing two rows of faultless white teeth.

"Shall I rob the Reichsbank, Mr. Hardt?" Hardt smiled. "You would succeed in that, too, Anderl. What have you there?"

The lad handed the engineer a folded paper. "A cablegram, Mr. Hardt. It came just before you arrived, and as it is from your uncle in America, I thought its contents must be important, so I kept it with me."

"Tommy Bighead?" said Hardt wonderingly as he read the message. Then suddenly he laughed out, as he recalled the scene of presenting the bottle of beer.

"Read it, Mr. Kamphenkel," he said, handing over the cablegram. "I am offered $250,000. Once again good old Uncle

Alex has put something over." He slapped Anderl on the back. "You don't need to rob the Reichsbank, Anderl. Everything is all fixed up."

VIII
PREPARATIONS FOR
A GREAT ADVENTURE

THE following days were marked by feverish activity on the eastern shore of Lake Constance. Hans Hardt did not wait for the arrival of the American before starting to build his great spaceship. He had immediately cabled his acceptance of Tommy Bighead's proposition. Under the terms of the agreement he had the advantage of adequate financial backing and could, at the same time, work without interference and without being held accountable to anyone. Kamphenkel was somewhat skeptical about accepting assistance under such unusual terms, but Hardt reassured him laughingly.

"Let the reporter write what he pleases," said he. "I'll not let him know what the world should not know. In any case, it will be convenient for me to have someone who will keep the newspaper people off my neck."

And so, the work of building was begun.

First, the construction plant acquired a strip or uncultivated land adjoining the lake. It extended from the shore of the lake eastward, mounting a slope which offered an excellent natural terrain for the take-off. Massive piles were driven into the depressions to make an even surface, over which strong steel tracks were built. Thus, in the course of time materialized a straight runway, forty feet wide by a mile and a quarter long, which extended from the proposed starting place, a few hundred yards along the level, gradually rising to terminate at the summit of the slope like a rampart.

Hardt passed hours daily supervising the workmen, checking

the solidity of the foundations, and testing in his laboratory the quality of the stone material. Meantime, in the various workshops, the individual parts of the spaceship were started. The work was at full swing when Tommy Bighead reached the scene of his campaign.

Hardt was so engrossed in his work that he had completely forgotten to meet his uncle and the foreign guest at the station. He was in the act of testing the rare metal beryllium, out of which he intended to make the prow of the spaceship, when he heard an automobile drive up before the laboratory.

"Go and see who is here, Anderl," he said to his assistant, without looking up from his work.

"Let them in or kick them out?" asked Anderl tersely.

"First see who it is."

Anderl stepped arrogantly forth to meet the newcomers. His face broke into a friendly grin as he recognized the small, slight figure, with two pipe-stems protruding from a coat pocket, which was Dr. Alexander Hardt.

"Welcome home, Doctor," he exclaimed.

"Come right in."

"Well, Anderl, how is everything?" asked Dr.

Hardt of the husky mechanic.

"Fine, thanks—Halt!" he suddenly broke in, as Bighead was about to enter. "That person stays out. No stranger can step foot in this laboratory."

Tommy Bighead, taking. the inevitable Havana cigar from his mouth, looked disdainfully at Anderl, and said in German, with his broad American accent: "Who let you out? Where I come from people dressed in such a clown's outfit would be locked up instead of running around loose."

This remark cut Anderl to the quick. "What do you mean, clown's outfit," he growled surlily, in his Bavarian dialect. "You don't know what a chamois leather suit is when you see one, you fool"

Tommy looked helplessly at his companion.

"What kind of a lingo does this man speak? I can't understand a word of it."

Fortunately, Hans Hardt appeared at that moment, and prevented Anderl from initiating Tommy further into the intricacies of the Bavarian dialect.

Anderl was annoyed at the hearty welcome bestowed by his chief upon Tommy, and he stalked moodily in after his master. Later on, when the American, on being formally introduced to him, slapped him condescendingly on the back as though he were a pet terrier, he turned away without a word, muttering imprecations under his breath. He could not so easily forgive the reporter's gibe at his clothes.

Inasmuch as Tommy was bent on getting information with which to start off his press campaign as promptly as possible, he soon brought the conversation around to the subject uppermost in his mind, the spaceship.

The laboratory disappointed him in its bare emptiness. The walls were covered with maps and charts. Near the window stood a massive work table covered with plans and blueprints. How, thought he to himself, could a prodigy of mechanical invention materialize from the maze of electrical connections attached to a marble slab and from the unpretentious-looking work bench covered with a tangle of wires, tubes and retorts.

"I cannot show you very much," Hardt began to explain, "but you will get a good general idea of .the project from the drawings and calculations."

"Never mind about the calculations, Mr. Hardt," protested Tommy. "I don't understand that sort of thing and my readers wouldn't be interested in it, But what about the alcohol?"

Hardt smiled.

"Do you know what a rocket is, Mr. Bighead?"

"Yes, of course. I have very frequently seen rockets in fireworks displays."

"Well, my spaceship will be no more than a rocket on a gigantic scale. Its explosive substance will be one of high valence. In a special chamber this substance will be slowly brought to combustion, and the gas thus generated will escape with violent force through small exhaust pipes, widening toward the end like funnels. Under the pressure resulting from these backward explosions, the rocket moves forward. As its movement depends solely upon pressure from the rear, the rocket is completely independent of the air through which it travels. In fact, it is in void space that the rocket gains its maximum power. That is really all there is to it."

"Fine! Any reader can understand that. But why hasn't somebody built such a rocket long ago, if it is so easy?"

"Well," laughed Hardt, "someone had to be the first to do it, and I happened to be that first one. The thing is not entirely simple, however. The great problem is the fuel, which must have an explosive power sufficient to give a speed of two and a half to three miles a second. The speed-producing explosives that have been known up to now are not sufficient. I happened to succeed in constructing a rocket which makes possible the use of a very effective liquid fuel."

"That's it! The alcohol!"

"Yes, alcohol. Denatured alcohol is a multivalent substance. In combination with the requisite oxygen-containing substance, which will produce the oxygen necessary for combustion, it is far superior to the chemical energy produced by the best nitrocellulose powder. The most effective fuel known till now is liquefied hydrogen, but it is very difficult to handle. Combined with oxygen, it produces oxyhydrogen gas, which is noted for its high explosive quality. The tanks of the rocket have to be filled with some multivalent fueL"

"Did you drive your flying machine across the ocean with such a rocket?"

"Certainly. As an experiment I built a number of rocket exhaust pipes into a large flying machine of the ordinary type used in our plant, instead of using motors and propeller. With this machine I reached a speed of two to two and a half miles a second. This was in empty space, of course, since such speed would be impossible in the atmosphere surrounding the earth. A fuel of such nature, however, will never be required for ordinary short-distance flying.

At a comparatively slow speed, the consumption of fuel would be disproportionately large, and the method consequently far too expensive. For great speed, with which the rocket motor begins to work economically," he paused for a moment and looked smilingly at the reporter, "our earth is too small."

"How so, too small? It would be a wonderful thing if it were possible to travel from New York to Cape Town in just a few minutes."

"Unfortunately that will never be possible. How can I explain this to you? Suppose that a gigantic cannon, stationed on a very high mountain, shoots out a ball in a horizontal direction. The projectile, under the influence of the earth's attraction, will follow a downward curving course until it strikes the earth. If the ball is shot upward with greater force, it will travel a longer distance because of the greater starting speed. Do you see that?"

"Yes. The greater the discharging force, the greater the distance covered in the flight."

"Correct. But this increase has a definite limit. Increase the initial speed to about four and a half miles a second, and the flight path will be so wide that it will extend around the world. The projectile will not reach the earth, but will, to a certain extent, fly in a continuous circular path, like a satellite around a planet. Should the starting speed increase to seven miles a second, the projectile will no longer be influenced by the earth's attraction. Do you see now why such high speed for earth flying is impossible?"

"It's a pity," commented Tommy. "Everything would be a spaceship if it only had a speed of seven miles a second."

"You have understood my explanation very well, Mr. Bighead. It is essentially a matter of producing this stupendous speed, and moreover, not suddenly as by means of a cannon, but so gradually that human beings will be able to endure the pressure. Only a rocket can accomplish this task. The exhaust pipes must work only until the traveling speed has reached the required rate. The work of the rocket is then finished, and the flying spaceship, without any driving impetus, proceeds on its course through the universe by its own momentum, like a projectile shot from a cannon.

"Do you believe it possible to produce a speed of seven miles a second?"

"I believe it is. During my experimental flight across the ocean my machine, with alcohol as a fuel, reached almost two and a half miles a second. With a few changes, my second machine will reach nearly three miles, and..."

"Isn't that fast enough?"

"This machine, being on the order of an airplane, would not be adapted for a trip into the Universe. The wings would be useless impedimenta in empty space. The alcohol fuel, while effective in flying through air, would not have sufficient power for space flying on account of its weight. The winged apparatus for the new rocket will serve merely as an auxiliary machine to start off the spaceship proper. When the auxiliary machine has reached its maximum speed of three miles a second, the rocket will detach itself from it. The rocket will have no air resistance to impede it and, with pure oxyhydrogen as a fuel, the speed of three miles will be easily increased by another four miles a second. While the auxiliary flying machine returns to earth with empty tanks, the wingless, oxyhydrogen-driven rocket carries onward the observation cabin with its occupants, past the circumscribing circle of the earth.

"Of the complete machine which starts from the earth, then, only a small part, the spacerocket, will mount to the moon, and only a sixtieth part of the original of that weight will return to the earth. If a great quantity of fuel were added to the weight of the indispensable equipment, it would be impossible safely to surmount the influence of the earth's gravity."

Tommy Bighead had listened closely to this explanation, and was cogitating as to what manner of article he could compose from the facts at hand. Meanwhile, Dr. Hardt had a query to put to his nephew.

"There is one thing I don't quite understand, Hans," he said, drawing vigorously on his pipe. "How can a human being exist in a spaceship when all normal conditions, like air, pressure, heat, and even the weight of one's body, are removed?"

"That is the least difficulty, Uncle Alex. I merely take a piece

49

of earth with me, which holds everything necessary to life, and, of course, tobacco for your beloved pipe as well. Ask, rather, how we will accomplish the exploration of the moon."

"What?" Tommy reentered the conversation. "Do you think you can land on the moon?"

"Not on the first trip. That has an exclusively scientific purpose, which is to observe phenomena. On the second expedition, however, I shall certainly attempt to land on the moon. The crew should, by all means, be able to leave the spaceship."

"On the moon, without any air?"

"Not alone on the moon, my dear sir, but during the free trip in space, should they be able to leave the spaceship!"

Tommy considered this a fantastic notion, but he politely remarked, "Isn't this a rather Utopian plan?"

Hardt opened the door of a small compartment built into the wall, completely lined with rubber and equipped with a pneumatic, air-tight lock. "There are two things," he said, " aside from the cold—which is conquerable—that cause men to consider existence in the void space beyond the earth impossible. These are the lack of pressure and the lack of air. I will now thin the air in this compartment with a rotation pump, so that the interior will become almost similar to airless and pressureless space."

The guest followed the movements of the engineer with great interest as he took a bundle from a drawer and unfolded it. "I have here an outfit of rubberized leather, similar to a diver's suit. It is completely air-tight. Through special chambers a certain amount of air will be continuously supplied, so that the pressure inside the suit will remain constant, unaffected by outside pressure conditions. Will one of you gentlemen be kind enough to wear this outfit? Unfortunately, I myself cannot carry out the experiment, as it will be necessary for me to attend to the exhaust."

Tommy Bighead examined the texture of the material and the detachable helmet, but drew back quickly as Hardt nodded encouragement to him. He much preferred to leave to Anderl the doubtful pleasure of being rabbit for the vivisector's knife.

In silent scorn at Tommy's reluctance, Anderl slipped into the suit, let Hardt screw on the heavy helmet with oxygen containers, and stationed himself in the center of the compartment. The heavy equipment would have crushed to the floor a less powerful frame than Anderl's.

Hardt gave him a lighted candle to hold in one leather-covered hand, and closed the door, through whose glass windows results could be observed. An electric bell, which Hardt had inserted in the compartment, could be distinctly heard outside.

The pump began to operate. The flame of the candle flickered and went out. The bell sounded gradually fainter until finally no sound could be heard, although the clapper continued to swing. Then Hardt disconnected the pump.

"The conditions now prevailing in this compartment are the same as those existing in space. There is no pressure and no air. In spite of that fact, my assistant apparently feels all right, although we cannot speak with him to find out."

As a matter of fact, Anderl's expression was rather peculiar. The suit was inflated, and reminded one of those rubber, air-filled figures so popular at the bathing beaches. The bulky, rotund form moved about in the compartment, swung its arms, and leaped into the air, so that there was no doubt of Anderl's being in full possession of his strength.

Hardt opened a small valve. Air whistled into the compartment; the bell sounded again; and the fantastic figure shrank into normal size. "With this diver's suit," remarked Dr. Hardt, as Anderl stripped off his cumbersome garb, "it will be possible to exist in airless space. But how, do you figure, can a man move in space when he is no longer subject to gravity and has no weight?"

"At first the lack of pressure will have a confusing effect upon the space traveler. That, however, will wear off as he becomes accustomed. Then it will not matter whether the people in the ship float about, weightless, in the air, or if they go about in the ordinary upright position. They will not miss their weight."

Tommy Bighead had maintained a bewildered silence for some time, and he was relieved when Dr. Hardt suggested departure. One question puzzled him still, however, and, as Hans Hardt was about to shake hands with him, he asked, "Mr. Hardt, what is your ultimate purpose with this invention?"

"My ultimate purpose?" repeated Hardt, leaning eagerly forward. "I will make available to the human race the inexhaustible heat energy of the sun. Far out in space, at the limit of the earth's gravitational influence, power stations shall come into existence, with enormous light reflectors which will make possible the concentration of great quantities of energy on any given point of the earth. It will thus come about that the hitherto frozen areas of the polar lands will be transformed into regions of productivity. Mankind will be unaffected by diminishing natural resources and will have no further need to take up arms. Plenty shall prevail on the earth, and a fortunate species of man shall be permitted to develop in unity and in liberty. This, Mr. Bighead, is the ultimate purpose of my invention."

Anderl beamed with pride at his master's significant statement. He then cast a look at Tommy Bighead which seemed to say, "There, what do you think of that, you ignoramus!"

Tommy merely said: "That's great, Mr. Hardt. It will make a nice little article for the *Michigan Evening Post*. Let's bet that the story will be on every news-stand in Detroit in an hour."

Dr. Hardt laughed. "You have forgotten, Mr. Bighead, that you are in Europe now."

"All right, then, in three hours," answered the reporter drily.

[

I X
THE MERRY-GO-ROUND

MONTHS passed. An unusually severe, but dry, winter favored the work on Lake Constance. In the midst of building process, Hardt came to the disturbing realization that he had underestimated the total cost of the project. Tommy cabled to Detroit and his firm came to the rescue with additional financial assistance. Such a response was in their own interest, however, since it was impossible for Tommy to secure a return on the investment, in press news, as long as the spaceship remained unfinished.

Hans Hardt was indefatigably active. He was relieved of his official duties as chief construction engineer of the plant, so that he could devote his entire time and energy to the building of the spaceship. It was due to his untiring efforts that, by the end of January, both the take-off field and the ship were nearing completion. He had set the crew to assembling the machine and had issued to his uncle a formal invitation to accompany him on the trip.

It was then that the scientist, past his youth though he was, hesitated, on the brink of his great venture. Certainly it was not fear that caused him to waver. It was rather a feeling of recoil before the prodigiousness of the undertaking, and the shrinking of a modest and retiring spirit before world renown. He was capable of mastering such feelings, however.

"Uncle Alex," said Hans, "if our trip into the Universe is to be profitable to science, there must be someone along who knows something of archeology, mineralogy and chemistry. Just think how much there is to discover on the old moon. Aside from that, it is essential that the occupants of the spaceship, who will live together in confined quarters for weeks, perhaps, understand each other thoroughly, as you and I do, for instance. Furthermore, your medical knowledge is indispensable."

Dr. Hardt's reluctance perceptibly weakened.

"All right, Hans," he finally said. "I'll go along. But don't you dare put up any 'No Smoking' signs in your illustrious world space cruise?"

Hardt selected Anderl as the third man, because he knew that the Bavarian was dependable under any circumstances.

To operate the auxiliary machine, which was to return to earth after its fuel was exhausted, Hardt chose two engineers whom he had trained especially for this work.

The last weeks before the start slipped rapidly by. Of primary importance was the testing of the five men to ascertain their fitness to endure conditions under which no human being had yet existed, and whose effects upon the individual could not be foreseen. Even if the lack of weight during the free trip in space caused no especially injurious effects, there remained the danger resulting from the enormous increase of pressure during the ascension.

In order to make such a test, Hardt built an apparatus much like a merry-go-round, in which the subjects were driven in a circular course at a terrific rate of speed. The centrifugal force produced an increasing pressure upon them, and its effects could be observed.

Hardt thought he had settled the question of who was to go on the trip, but he had not reckoned with Tommy Bighead's determination to be a member of the party. "It is out of the question, Mr. Bighead," he had said emphatically to Tommy, who felt indignant at not being included among the three men invited to take the rocket trip.

"Then that Anderl must be left behind," insisted Tommy.

"Why, you haven't any of the knowledge necessary to take Anderl's place. Each member of. the party must be qualified to drive the ship in my stead at any time. Moreover, we will find ourselves in situations where the least mistake would mean certain death for all of us."

"Well, I'll take lessons. I'm an expert automobile driver, and I've already driven one flying machine. I know I can do it."

"I do not doubt your ability, but the time is too short for instructing you. We are to start in ten days. Besides, grateful as I am to you for raising the money for the expedition, I hardly think you are physically fit. Just drop the idea, Mr. Bighead."

"No," said Tommy positively. "I want to go along—I have to go along so that I can write articles and earn back the money your machine cost. You can't refuse me this."Tommy, puffing thick clouds of smoke from his cigar, appeared resolute in his determination.

Hardt perceived that he could not dissuade the American from his idea by means of words. "Very well," he said. "If you are physically strong enough, I will take you instead of Anderl. You will have to be tested."

Tommy laughed disdainfully. Indeed, he did not look like any weakling.

"All right," he agreed. "Shall I slaughter a bull with my bare hands?"

Hardt smiled. "There would hardly be occasion for that in space. Come over here to the pressure tester instead."

Hardt called Anderl. The latter frowned furiously when he realized what was going on. He dared not object, however, and tramped gloomily ahead.

The testing apparatus had been built on a vacant, level plot of ground. It was composed of a strong steel bar, sixty feet in length, which rotated from the center next the ground, like the hand of a clock. At each end of the powerful "clock hand" hung, in a strong frame, a small, padded gondola. The gondola was suspended into a circular groove surrounding the prescribed space. As the steel bar rotated, the gondolas moved through the groove like the seats of a merry-go-round. The faster the merry-go-round revolved, the greater was the effect upon the passengers of the pressure created by the centrifugal force. The electromotor, by which the apparatus was run, could be operated from a switchboard outside the circle.

Hardt made a few test rotations, of the apparatus and then invited the American to step into one of the gondolas.

"This apparatus, Mr. Bighead, will decide impartially between you and Anderl. I will gradually increase the speed, and the one of you who can endure the pressure the longest will go on the trip to the moon. Agreed?"

"All right," said Tommy, and he stepped in.

This new kind of duel seemed to amuse him.

Anderl, who had already settled himself comfortably in the opposite gondola, looked over the edge of the groove and called out, "Will it make any difference to you, sir, if I come to your funeral in my chamois suit?"

Tommy threw Anderl a look of utter disdain before settling down according to Hardt's directions.

"As soon as the pressure becomes too great for you, Mr. Bighead, push down this lever. It shuts off the motor."

"There's no danger of my letting this fellow outdo me," said Tommy confidently.

"I would urge that you do not wait too long," cautioned the engineer earnestly. "The pressure slows up the heart action, and even the best reporter in the State of Michigan can't write articles after he is dead."

Tommy made a gesture of protest and said: "Don't you worry," which meant, in this case, "There's no use trying to scare me out." "Breathe as evenly and as deeply as you can."

"Let her go!" ordered Tommy.

Hardt turned away with a shrug, started the motor, and the steel bar began to move. Anderl sang lustily, as though riding on a merry-go-round at a fair. He winked slyly at his chief. Tommy lay motionless in the gondola.

Faster and faster circled the apparatus. The tachometer on the switchboard indicated five, eight, ten revolutions a minute. The centrifugal force thus produced brought the gondolas out of the grove into an oblique position.

Hardt pushed the lever farther. At sixteen revolutions a minute the counter pressure was almost two and a half times that of the earth, and was equal to that which would be produced in the rocket by normal functioning of the exhaust pipes. The gondolas rushed through the air with a whistling sound.

Anderl had become silent.

Hardt kept this speed for a time in order to accustom the contestants to the pressure. Then he cautiously pushed the lever still further. He shook his head in concern when, at twenty revolutions, neither Tommy nor Anderl had used the emergency lever. The pressure was now at about the limit of human endurance. The gondolas were swung out in a position almost horizontal with the steel bar, and circled through the groove at a dizzy speed. At twenty-two revolutions a minute Hardt dared not further increase the speed. It was obvious that both numskulls would, rather have their bones crack than give in...He shut off the motor. The circling gondolas immediately dropped into normal position and came gradually to a standstill as the machine stopped moving.

There came no sign of life from the gondolas.

Anderl blinked up composedly at the engineer, though he was breathing heavily. In comparison with Anderl, Tommy was in a grievous plight. His face had turned blue, and his body twitched convulsively. He had not suffered any serious effects, however, and within a few minutes he had recovered to the extent of being able to crawl clumsily out of the gondola with Hardt's assistance. Reeling like a drunken man, he stood, stiff-legged, looking around in bewilderment at the crinkly world through which he had to find his way.

Anderl staggered a trifle, too, but he came abruptly to his senses on catching sight of his rival.

"Have you had enough, little friend from America?" he inquired almost cordially.

Tommy looked hard at his opponent. Little by little his face assumed an expression of intelligence, and he became articulate.

"Well!" he uttered thickly. "I've won!" Anderl laughed in derision. "You look it," he scoffed. "Of course you could have stood it longer yet with the disconnection. It was only just becoming agreeable!"

"Hold on," interrupted Hardt. "Neither of you has been tested with the disconnection. The test is incomplete in that respect. The immediate question is who has best stood the pressure.

Tommy looked at Anderl, who appeared as fresh as though nothing had happened. "I object," he said as firmly as his condition permitted. "It wasn't fair!"

"What's that you're saying? Hardt and I are swindlers, are we?"

With threatening mien Anderl advanced toward the reporter and, before Hardt could interfere, he had raised his arm to strike Tommy in the face. Realizing the sorry condition of the American, however, he let his fist drop to his side.

"Very well," said he, relenting. "I'll let you live a while longer. But you can't go on the trip. Do you understand?"

Tommy understood Anderl's gesture better than his words. His wrath gave him renewed strength.

"I can fight, too," he snarled, as his fist landed on Anderl's leather breeches.

That was too much for Anderl. "Just wait, you insignificant little shrimp!" he retorted angrily. "I'll show you who has a wishbone where his backbone ought to be!"

Like lightning he seized Tommy's wrists and pressed them together with such force that Tommy sank to his knees with a groan.

This happened so quickly that Hardt had no opportunity to prevent it. "Let go, Anderl!" he commanded furiously. "What in Heaven's name has gotten into you!"

"Who won the test," asked Anderl, without yielding, "he or I?"

Hardt suppressed a smile. Tommy hung so limp and helpless in Anderl's giant fist that it was impossible, with the most charitable intentions, to decide in the American's favor.

"Mr. Bighead," he said, as Anderl loosened his grip, "the test showed inconclusive results. Shall we repeat it?"

Tommy painfully lifted himself to an erect posture. "No!" he said curtly, and turned away in silence.

Anderl had won the trip. From that time on, however, Tommy Bighead was his implacable enemy.

X
THE TAKE-OFF

AT last came the long-anticipated day of departure. Hans Hardt had particularly requested Tommy Bighead not to announce the time of the take-off, in order to escape annoyance, but somehow the news leaked out. On the morning of February eight, the take-off field was completely surrounded with a crowd of cameramen, newspaper reporters and curious spectators, who frequently slipped through the barriers in an attempt more closely to inspect the spaceship. The guards whom Tommy had stationed at the field were hustling away, none too gently, any reporter who could not identify himself with a pass. Tommy himself was besieged by information seekers from all nations, and a long queue of newspaper representatives in front of his lodging quarters anxiously waited for news.

Anderl spent the day in a final inspection of the individual parts of the intricate machine and in storing the cabins with the appropriate baggage and food supplies which had been exactly proportioned. He put on board, also, a tiny cage containing a yellowish green canary, twittering with fright. Anderl knew that Hardt loved this little bird and took pleasure in hearing it sing during leisure hours.

Hans Hardt and his uncle remained in seclusion during this, their last day on earth. They went out onto the lake in a small boat. Both men gazed for a long time at the snow-covered woods and hills encompassing the lake. They said a silent farewell, not only to the hills, but to Mother Earth in general, to terra firma, to air and heat, to the sway of man on earth.

What would come with the approaching hours and days? Would they succeed or would they fail? Would they ever again breathe this air, feel the green grass under their feet, inhale the fragrance of blossoming springtime? Or was there rather in store for them a hideous death in the cold solitude of total darkness?

Hans Hardt shook himself free of these morbid thoughts which were threatening to break down his morale in this unforgettable hour of leave-taking.

"We must succeed!" he exclaimed to himself, looking at his watch.

Meantime, the crowd around the take-off field was increasing. Hour after hour the people patiently waited for the great event. In spite of repeated efforts, they could see nothing more than the huge hangar which sheltered the spaceship. Emerging from the hangar was the runway, whose tracks on their embankment extended like a railroad to the summit of the hill at the east.

The early dusk of a winter's day was setting in as Hans Hardt drove up to the field. With him in the car were Dr. Alexander Hardt, Tommy Bighead and Mr. Kamphenkel. Tommy's expression indicated an inner struggle, although he maintained complete silence. Now and then he smiled as though amused at some private joke. Yet, if questioned, he gave preoccupied and evasive replies.

A murmur passed through the crowd as the car broke through the line.

Anderl, in the inevitable leather breeches, stepped up to Hardt and reported, "Clear for the take-off." Hardt thanked him briefly and entered the hangar, brightly illuminated by the searchlights.

There rested the titanic spaceship. It was in the form of a blunted torpedo, with windows the entire length of its sides. Between the steel stabilizers at the stern yawned the opening of the huge main exhaust. The rocket proper was attached to a large winged machine, the exhausts of which were mounted in the wings like those of the machine Hardt had driven across the Atlantic. The men working on the enormous hull of the fantastic ship appeared like ants.

At a sign from Hardt the doors of the hangar sprang open. The dazzling rays of the searchlights shot forth into the darkness. The machine, on a series of roller trucks, moved slowly forward as though pushed by some invisible power, and glided out onto the runway.

A roaring cheer arose from the spectators as the colossal monster emerged from the hangar. It came to a standstill, but the interior was seething with activity. Lights flashed through the round windows; doors slammed; rope ladders were lowered to the ground.

The crowd below looked on in awed silence.

Here, materialized, was the fabulous machine, whose fame had been spread by the newspapers for months past. This was the skyship, fashioned of aluminum and beryllium, destined to carry three intrepid human souls on their mission to conquer the astral Universe. The thousand year dream of the human race was here at last converted into reality.

Was it possible that human intellect and human genius could prevail over the invincible forces of the earth and sun? Could they withstand the onslaught of those demons inhabiting the realms of nothingness? Could they actually bridge the dread abyss of cosmic space?

Hardt personally conducted a, few press men, carefully selected by Tommy, up a rope ladder to the rocket.

Just back of the prow shone in large gold letters the name *Wieland.* "That's a mighty clever name," remarked one of the group. "*Wieland,* a legendary smith, is the prototype of our modern engineer. His name, therefore, symbolizes skill and courage."

The port window in the outer wall led to a cabin just large enough to hold two men. "This entrance," explained the engineer, "is the only one through which the interior rooms of the rocket are accessible. Both doors being air-tight, it is possible to leave the ship in space without causing any change in the air pressure of the interior. In making the exit, one passes through the inner door into the cabin. He closes the inner door and then opens the outer one."

Passing through the cabin, the guests entered an electrically illuminated chamber, shaped like a truncated cone horizontally placed.

"This is the observation cabin," continued Hardt. "There is a room of the same size below, of which half is used for sleeping quarters and half for a kitchen."

"Below?" queried one of the journalists in a surprised tone.

"Oh, yes," Hardt hastened to reply. "I must first explain what is meant in this ship by 'below' and 'above.' According to Nature's law, the direction of 'below' is determined by the effect of pressure, which is, of course, toward the center of the earth. As soon as our exhaust pipes begin to function, however, the pressure is effective from the ship's prow toward the exhaust. Thus, in our language, the prow is always 'above' and the stern 'below.' This sounds strange to you with the ship resting in a horizontal position, and in a room of this unusual shape. During the ascent this cabin, now horizontal, becomes vertically erect, and what now appears to be a flat circular wall, becomes the floor. Our flight path, for the most part, will be either partially or wholly unaffected by the earth's attraction, and in consequence there will be no actual 'above' and 'below.' That is why you don't find any stairs in this ship, but only light rope ladders which can be adjusted according to our position. Without gravity, stationary stairs would be useless obstructions. Numerous hand grips on the floors and walls will be our most effective means of moving about. During the ascent, when there will be a powerful downward pressure, it will be unnecessary to move."

The visitors walked cautiously around the curved, many-windowed observation cabin, examining it with curious interest.

"I shall not have time to explain to you in detail the numerous devices that you see attached to the various walls and partitions," said Hardt. "All the recording instruments, which are run by electric current, have their connections on the main switchboard. Instead of this compass, which is more or less useless to us, a gyroscope shows at any time our ship's static position and any changes in its direction. Three compression springs, corresponding to the three coordinates of the room, give the rate of acceleration. Other instruments automatically deduct the speed from the rate of acceleration compared with the time, and the distance covered. That row of scales, connected with various parts of the ship, consists of built-in manometers and barometers of outside pressure and atmospheric conditions. These levers control fuel pumps, the starter and the ignition. The ship can be controlled with the slightest shifting of the levers.

"The most important part of the machine is this strong lever regulating the introduction of fuel into the combustion chamber. The scale above it indicates the absolute rate of acceleration. The bright red line appearing on the scale is the border line between life and death. As long as the rate of acceleration is under one hundred and thirty feet per second, there is no immediate danger for the crew. The minute the indicator goes beyond that conspicuous mark, death from the extreme pressure may be the result."

The guests looked awed as they inspected the scale and lever, and took good care not to touch anything.

Charts with transversal lines, for registering curves in accordance with the figures shown on the various scales, were suspended on revolving pedestals. Every inch of available space on the walls was utilized.

"In the front, or, according to our ship vocabulary, above," said Hardt, "are three tightly folded parachutes, each with a surface of about 400 square feet. In case of such an emergency, as the machine not responding to control, these parachutes would protect the members of the crew in the steep descent. I trust, however, that we shall never have occasion to use them."

"Won't you show us the other rooms, Mr. Hardt?"

"What other rooms? The sleeping room and the tiny kitchen which holds our supplies cannot possibly interest you."

"But surely a ship of this size must contain more than a couple of cabins, which are very small in proportion to the body of the W ieland."

"Of course," replied Hardt with a smile.

"The rest of the hull is occupied by tanks of fuel, oxyhydrogen gas. These tanks are inaccessible from the inside. And now I am sorry," he said, looking at his watch, "but I must ask you to leave the ship. It is nearly six o'clock, and we leave in thirty minutes."

This request was obeyed reluctantly. There were many

unanswered questions concerning ventilation, temperature, steering, course of flight, and so on. Hardt refused to give any further information, however, and insisted on an immediate clearance of the ship.

As he reappeared at the entrance, he was greeted with a burst of applause. After a fruitless effort to silence the crowd, he abandoned his intention of making a brief farewell speech, and took leave of the various guests of honor with hearty handshakes.

But where was Tommy Bighead all this time?

Hardt sent a man to search for him, but to no avail. Tommy had disappeared.

"He cannot recover from his chagrin at being left behind instead of Anderl," remarked Hardt to his uncle in some irritation, as the latter climbed into the ship.

"It seems strange," replied Dr. Hardt. "I can understand his feeling disappointed, but that doesn't excuse him from seeing us off."

Hardt shrugged his shoulders. "Well, I cannot wait for Mr. Tommy Bighead. Every moment of delay in starting upsets the calculations for our course." Whereupon he gave a few final instructions to the pilot of the auxiliary machine and disappeared into the ship.

Anderl threw off the rope ladders. The entrance closed automatically. The spectators gazed in amazed silence at the monstrous machine, dully gleaming in the rays of the searchlights. Presently a loud report sounded. It was the signal for the take-off.

The spaceship began to vibrate. A sudden, deafening roar caused the people to duck their heads in fright. The exhaust pipes had begun to operate and were spitting forth flaming gas. Slowly, at first, the ship taxied along the tracks of the runway. A moment more, and it broke loose like a wild demon. Faster and faster it tore ahead. In half a second it was charging up the slope at a furious speed; ten seconds and the mile mark was past. Then— then, like some incredibly gigantic dragonfly, it lifted itself free of the trucks and floated out into the night.

What a spectacle! From the brilliantly illuminated field the serried crowd of spectators sent a thundering cheer after the ascending spaceship. As though lifted by invisible hands, the fiery creation mounted on its mad course toward the heavens.

A series of loud explosions rent the air. Panic stricken, the crowd scattered, then paused to stare at the fantastic spectacle above them. The auxiliary machine was operating under full fuel, and the exhaust pipes opening along the edge of the wings were emitting a wide sheaf of flame which trailed out like the tail of a comet behind the speeding ship.

A tiny spark of light was floating downwards above the hills on the east shore of the lake. It was a parachute carrying a farewell message from the fleeting *Wieland*. It went unnoticed, for the time being, as all eyes were fixed on the man-made comet sweeping across the sky.

The take-off field sank in to darkness as the fiery trail of the ship receded into the distance and the searchlights were extinguished. In scarcely five minutes the machine was visible only as a dim point of light above the southeastern horizon.

Kamphenkel looked at his watch. "Two hundred and eighty seconds," he said to his neighbor. "Hans Hardt has just disconnected the spacerocket from the auxiliary flying machine and turned on the oxyhydrogen gas."

"How far is he by now?"

"He must be five hundred miles away."

"Incredible!" exclaimed the journalist. "In five minutes from Lake Constance to Vienna?"

"Yes," replied Kamphenkel, pale with excitement. "Supposing someone had told us ten years ago that such a thing could be possible! The *Wieland* is now reaching the limit of the earth's atmospheric circle. The auxiliary machine has played its role and will descend somewhere in the vicinity of Vienna or Budapest."

Powerful field glasses enabled the observers to watch the spaceship for a few minutes. Presently, however, the point of light completely disappeared.

"It doesn't seem possible!" exclaimed Kamphenkel on his way home. "Just a few minutes ago I was standing inside the machine.

Now it is soaring through space, an infinitesimal fragment of the earth, somewhere betwixt here and the moon."

On the following morning the newspapers published detailed accounts of the take-off and the course that the spaceship would follow. "If last night," the story ran, "astronomical observatories were unable to follow the receding point of light which was the *Wieland*, let it be no cause for alarm. The small amount of light radiated by the rocket is too feeble to be perceived through even our most powerful telescopes. The *Wieland* will become visible only when it leaves the shadow of the earth and reflects the light of the sun."

As a matter of fact, the next evening, at exactly the same hour as that of the take-off on the preceding evening, the *Wieland* reappeared in the eastern sky. Even then, however, she was not visible through small telescopes and other optical instruments. The public had to depend on the reports of large astronomical observatories, whose enormous reflectors enabled the detection of the *Wieland* as a tiny speck of light floating in the aphelion distance, amounting to about fifteen times the diameter of the earth.

Exactly like a star, it mounted higher, passed through the meridian, sank towards the southwest, and finally, towards morning, disappeared beyond the horizon. The same thing happened the following night. Before touching the southwestern horizon, however, the little speck of light abruptly disappeared.

The public was seized with panic. Reports from all the prominent observatories consistently stated that the *Wieland* could no longer be discerned on the firmament.

In hope alternating with dread, Kamphenkel waited for the next night. Again the spaceship failed to appear in the heavens. The large observatories could offer no reassurance.

What had happened? Had the Universe claimed its sacrifice? The world shuddered. Hans Hardt and his loyal companions, lost, forever!

XI
EN ROUTE
TO THE MOON

SHORTLY before the first projecting stage of the journey Anderl threw down the rope ladder. He carefully closed the hatches and then hastened into the control room.

There stood Hans Hardt in front of the main switchboard, watching the chronometer. His keen gaze traveled from shining instruments and switchboard levers to the large charts mapping their course.

"Where is Dr. Hardt?" he asked.

"Putting his cabin in order," was the reply.

"Do you want me to call him?"

Hardt nodded and lay down in a hammock, so hung that all the principal levers could be operated from it. The mat, previously covering the curved floor, had been removed. During the ascent, when the pressure produced by their speed counterbalanced that of the earth's gravity, this floor was to become a wall. The round surface now at the rear would then constitute the floor of the cabin.

Dr. Hardt appeared.

"It is really quite a comfortable room down there, Hans, and I feel at home in it already. It is, of course, a trifle cramped. Besides I have to get used to such an airy roost, but…"

"If you want to take in the ascent," interrupted Hardt, "get into that hammock as fast as you can. The exhaust pipes will start to work in two minutes. It will be too bad for anyone hanging around here after that. Take off all unnecessary clothing."

Dr. Hardt obediently removed his coat and climbed into the

hammock, a trifle frightened at the approaching ordeal.

"Everything all right?" Hardt inquired by telephone of the pilot of the auxiliary machine.

"All is ready," came the calm reply.

"Good. Start at exactly thirty-two minutes and forty seconds after six."

The engineer gave his orders with quiet firmness, as though this were an ordinary journey. There was not the slightest tremor of excitement in his voice at this fateful moment. After a final glance at his two companions in the hammocks, he concentrated his attention on the chronometer. Six thirty-two, and the second hand crept around—five, ten seconds.

Dr. Hardt peeped out the window. There was the take-off field, the milling crowd, whose upturned faces in the brilliant light revealed tense emotion. No outside sound, however, could penetrate the hermetically sealed ship. Only the steady pounding of the electric motor and the shrill whine of the generator were audible from the center of the ship.

The second hand passed twenty-thirty. Dr. Hardt stared at this hand as though hypnotized. It crept inexorably ahead, second by second. There was no going back now.

The events of the last few months flashed through his mind—his nephew's hardships, the search for alcohol in America, the ocean flight, Tommy Bighead, the smartest reporter in Michigan—from where else could he be, this determined American?

A smile froze on Dr. Hardt's face. A noise like thunder vibrated through the ship. The hammocks swayed; the chronometer needle swung back to zero. The trip into the Universe had begun.

The take-off field flashed by the window. For a moment Dr. Hardt glimpsed handkerchiefs and hats being waved above the crowd; then gleaming treetops, the roofs of Friedrichshafen, and the glistening surface of Lake Constance in the background. All this was left behind.

The ship had risen beyond the runway and soared into the air. The dull illumination from the ground faded into total blackness.

Hardt took up the telephone. "Full gas!" was the command to

the auxiliary machine. Immediately the roar of the exhaust pipes grew louder. The acceleration meter indicated an increase of sixty-five feet a second. The springs fastening the hammocks stretched with an ominous creak, and the cords tightened about the body, which was double its former weight.

Dr. Hardt lay wearily gazing upward. It was weird to see the windows, through which he had but recently watched the starry sky, sink downwards, while the curved wall moved up to bar his view. He turned his head with an effort. The concave wall now surrounded him on every side. Above and below was a flat, round surface. The frustum of the cone had taken its upright position. Thirty seconds passed thus.

"Hans!" gasped Dr. Hardt. "Yes, Uncle Alex."

"Is everything really all right? It seems so heavy."

"It is only the pressure, Uncle Alex."

"Do you see that strange formation of stars over there at a level with us, surrounded by a haze?"

Hardt glanced through the window. "Formation of stars?" He looked at the altimeter. "That formation of stars is very probably Munich."

Greatly astonished, Dr. Hardt attempted to rise, but was thrown heavily back by the pressure.

"Munich?" he said weakly. "Are you out of your mind? Since when do cities cling to the sky?"

"Don't ask questions, Uncle Alex, but breathe as deeply as you can. It will soon be worse."

After four minutes the acceleration needle began to move back.

"The auxiliary machine has nearly exhausted its fuel, Anderl. We must soon disconnect."

Anderl already had his hand on the lever.

Hardt looked at the speedometer. "Only two and a half miles a second," he said to himself, shaking his head. By telephone he said good-by to the pilot of the auxiliary machine, after which he directed Anderl to disconnect.

A light pressure, and the space rocket freed itself from the auxiliary machine. Simultaneously Hardt's hand reached for the

• Otto Willi Gail

starting lever.

"Now is the time. Don't forget the breathing.".

He pushed the lever. The ship gave a tremendous jerk. The exhaust pipes were in operation.

Once more the acceleration needle was moving forward-to sixty-five, eighty, one hundred, paused at one hundred and five. The ship's speed was increasing by one hundred and five feet a second. At one hundred and thirty the red line was reached.

The pressure was becoming intolerable. Dr. Hardt attempted to lift his hand, but it fell heavily back to his side. Every limb seemed weighted, as though held down by four strong men. Mercury, instead of blood, seemed to flow through his veins. The cords of the hammock cut so deeply through the pillows that they bruised his back. He was not asking questions now. It was enough to struggle for air, with lungs that were scarcely able to lift the burden off his chest. Resisting this great heaviness for a time, he attempted to cry out, to say something, no matter what. Discouraged at last, he sank back. His thoughts wandered.

Hans, too, was greatly affected by the pressure. The few simple operations to be performed at the switchboard, ordinarily within the power of a child, now required every ounce of his strength. It was a great effort merely to stretch his arm to the lever.

The speedometer registered three and a half miles a second. The violent noise of the exhaust had ceased, for the ship was traveling at an altitude where the extraordinarily thin air could not transmit sound. Hans pushed the gas lever further. The *Wieland* was working up to capacity, spitting forth its glowing vapors with stupendous power. The needle approachd the red line. After two minutes the speed was reached which was to carry the ship beyond the confines of the earth. The speedometer needle crawled steadily ahead—four, four and a half miles a second.

A terrifying thought flashed through the mind of the engineer. What if he should lose the strength to move back the lever? The speed would increase until the oxyhydrogen gas stored in the reserve tanks was exhausted. With no fuel, return to earth be impossible. The *Wieland*, beyond influence. by the earth, would career madly through planetary space, on a course leading into the infinite. In a quarter of an hour's time, the ship's speed would suffice to carry her through the solar system.

Seven minutes had elapsed. The machine roared on at five miles a second. Slowly and painfully Hardt lifted his arm and placed it in a sling suspended from the ceiling. Only a few inches intervened between his fingers and the lever. I t cost him enormous effort to move his hand even a fraction of an inch. He paused for a moment in exhaustion. He must not collapse now! The speedometer needle moved with relentless precision to five and a half miles. Only three more seconds remained. With a last convulsive effort his hand seized the lever and pushed it back. Completely exhausted by the terrific exertion, he sank back, his forehead covered with perspiration.

The acceleration needle moved back now, until it finally settled at a steady decrease of ten feet a second. The pressure ceased as suddenly as it had started. The chronometer registered eight minutes.

XII
THE EARTH
IN PERSPECTIVE

N the control room of the *Wieland* reigned complete silence, broken only by the heavy breathing of the three men. Dr. Hardt opened his eyes and looked about him. The lights were on, and the windows looked out on utter blackness. The heaviness had departed from his limbs and his effort to rise this time was successful. It was pleasant to have control of his muscles and to move about once more. He experienced a sense of great relief like that of a person awakening from a nightmare.

"Hans," he called, "where are we now?" "Will you please come here, Doctor?" answered Anderl's gruff voice.

Dr. Hardt climbed out of his hammock and proceeded with cautious and uncertain steps toward his nephew's hammock. He found great difficulty in keeping his balance. It seemed he was about to fall forward at every step. What had come over him? He felt peculiarly light.

Perhaps it was merely a normal reaction from the terrific pressure which had left his muscles aching.

Hans Hardt lay bathed in perspiration. Anderl, in much anxiety, was rubbing his temples. Dr. Hardt held a bottle of camphor under his nose. He slowly opened his eyes and looked without recognition at his companions. In a few seconds, however, he regained consciousness. His first impulse was to look at the chronometer. It registered twelve minutes.

"The hammocks can be put away now," he said to Anderl, as he sprang up and began to study the curves plotted by the instruments.

"What a trip that was!" exclaimed Dr. Hardt.

"As long as I live I shall never forget those eight minutes. Every bone in my body aches," he said, gingerly feeling of various parts of his anatomy. "It seems, though, that they are all intact."

"Yes, no human being could indefinitely survive such pressure," replied the engineer. "Anderl, will you go and see if everything is all right below?"

"Hans," queried Dr. Hardt, as Anderl disappeared, "were are we now?"

Hardt consulted the recordings of the instruments. "We have covered three thousand, seven hundred and fifty miles and are at an altitude of two thousand five hundred."

"Great heavens!" exclaimed the scientist.

"We are four hundred times higher than Mount Everest, the highest point of the earth."

"Yes. The barometers on the exterior are not registering. We left terrestrial regions long ago, and now we are soaring in the Universe."

Anderl reappeared and reported that all was well.

"That's good, Anderl. You go to sleep now, and in six hours you can take my place here."

"If I must, Mr. Hardt," said Anderl, with disappointment in his tone.

"Of course you must, Anderl. Don't worry. There will be nothing but darkness to see for a long time yet. Have a good sleep, Anderl."

Dr. Hardt stood peering out the window. "I can't see a thing of the earth, Hans."

Hardt stepped to his side and adjusted the telescope. "If you look closely, you will see a gleam of light from time to time, perhaps a searchlight from some tower, or the signal of some steamer which is struggling through the ocean down there."

"Ocean?"

"If it were light, we could now see the earth from the Philippines to the east coast of France. At present we are apparently directly above the Arabian Sea."

"Please focus the telescope on a city. I should like to see how..."

Hardt laughed merrily. "That is asking too much, Uncle Alex." He adjusted the telescope. "In approximately this direction should lie the Indian Ocean. Perhaps you can locate the reflection of the lights of Bombay. I hope you succeed. But don't think you are going to observe Hindu night life from here."

The telescope was pointing in an almost horizontal direction, with a slightly downward inclination.

"I want to see the earth, Hans, not Mars."

"All right. Take off your glasses and look through the telescope."

Dr. Hardt drew back in surprise. "What do you mean? The earth is down there." He made an agitated gesture toward the floor.

Hardt smiled. "Certainly. There is Lake Constance. "

"Well, and?..."

"And where do you think we are to look for the center of the earth?"

"The center of the earth? I haven't been there yet, but I should judge that it is deeper than Lake Constance."

"Naturally. Where else?"

"Over there, Uncle Alex." Hardt pointed through the window. "There is the center of the earth, and above it the Arabian Sea, which is directly opposite us at this moment."

Dr. Hardt stared in astonishment. "The earth up there, where the sky should be?"

"Don't forget," Hardt explained, "that we ascended from the earth in an oblique direction. We, therefore, have to look for that planet in front of us rather than below us. The pressure which places the axis of the ship in a vertical position does not come from the earth but from our rocket's exhaust pipes, which are still operating with slight force."

The Doctor was somewhat confused.

"If we had ascended from the other side of the earth where the sun was shining," Hardt added, "we would now be able to see the surface of the earth from the side. The northwest section of the globe would lie at our feet; the southeast section would appear from a horizontal direction, and the whole visible surface would be at an angle of nearly ninety degrees. I am sorry I am not able to show you such a marvelous view."

"Why didn't we make the ascent in the day-time?"

"On account of the observations to be made from the earth by the astronomical observatories. Otherwise, we would make the entire trip between the earth and the sun; but we would not be visible from the earth."

Hardt busied himself with the charts of their course, leaving his uncle to his own thoughts concerning this unique position of theirs. He gazed out into space, trying to realize that in the far distance lay terra firma, where human beings were walking to and fro, little troubled by the question as to whether their legs were directed toward the center of the earth.

After a moment Dr. Hardt broke the silence. "There are probably hundreds of thousands of people watching us now, gazing after a disappearing point of light. When I think of all the frozen feet and the colds which will develop down there to-morrow, all on our account, it seems to me a matter of courtesy to make some sign of recognition. You act as though you don't care about Mother Earth any longer."

"Good old Uncle Alex," replied Hardt, with a smile. "The recordings of my instruments are indeed of far greater interest and importance than the darkness yonder. It will suffice if you take over that conventional duty, though not because of the cold feet, I hope."

"Quite the contrary. I find it uncomfortably hot here," complained Dr. Hardt. "Can you shut off the steam?"

"I'm sorry to say I can't. The heat is coming from the outside."

"From the outside? I thought it would be terribly cold in the Universe."

"Of course. This heat, however, developed from the friction of the air against the surface of our ship. We can feel thankful that the beryllium prow stood up so well. For your consolation I can assure you that this great heat will not last much longer. Incidentally, it has already cooled off considerably."

Hardt called to Anderl, who had not yet gone to 'sleep. "What does the thermometer show down there?"

"Ninety-one degrees Fahrenheit," came the reply.

"H-m! The thermometer up here shows one hundred degrees," said Hardt. "Anderl, we will turn on some fluid oxygen and then open the valves regulating the overpressure for a little while."

The heat was indeed oppressive, and the evaporating oxygen brought only moderate relief.

Dr. Hardt yawned. "I am extremely tired," he said, wiping his brow. "I don't know why, but I feel just as though I had spent a wakeful night, and we have been on our way scarcely half an hour."

"Go and lie down, Uncle Alex," urged Hardt, realizing that the heat was not the only cause of his uncle's weariness. "When you wake up again, these disagreeable symptoms, which were a parting gift of the earth, will have disappeared."

Dr. Hardt climbed heavily down the rope ladder into the sleeping quarters. The wide, inviting hammock seemed to him at that moment the greatest invention of all times. Before he had finished undressing, he fell into the hammock and went immediately into a deep, dreamless sleep.

Hardt remained at his post, although he, too, had to fight against the breath-taking heat and a tremendous lassitude in his limbs. As long as the *Wieland* soared within the regions of terrestrial magnetism, he could not trust anyone else with the observation of the instruments. It was essential to collect data for his contemplated landing maneuvers, and the slightest error in calculations could result in very serious consequences. From time to time he moved still farther back the lever controlling the rate of acceleration. The incessant activity of the exhaust pipes correspondingly decreased, and as a consequence the pressure diminished. Everything began to lose weight. He could have shut off the rocket altogether, for they had long ago reached the speed required to carry them safely beyond the earth's influence. He dared not, however, bring about too suddenly this complete freedom from gravity which would result from disconnecting the exhaust pipes. It was necessary to accustom himself and his companions very gradually to conditions whose effects were so far unpredictable. He was especially concerned over the consumption of fuel, which was diminishing more rapidly than he had calculated. He could think of no satisfactory explanation for this. In order to conserve the fuel that was left, he throttled to an increasing extent the discharges of the rocket.

The night advanced. The chronometer indicated that they had been on their way for six hours. Forty-three thousand, seven hundred and fifty miles, almost double the circumference of the earth, separated the space travelers from their fellow beings. They were still flying through total darkness. The earth was invisible; only a wide, starless area amidst the constellations of the zodiac indicated the location of their own planet.

"Now the printing machines are busily turning off the morning papers," mused Hardt to himself. "Probably Tommy Bighead has slept very little all night."

The ship continued to radiate its heat into outer space. The occupants felt more cheerful with the feeling of increased freedom. The engineer smiled as he thought of the surprises which were in store for his passengers. Finally, as the *Wieland* was out of danger for the time being, he lay down to rest.

XIII
THE UNIVERSE

WHEN Dr. Hardt awoke, he found himself alone in the sleeping compartment. Looking at his watch, he speculated as to whether it was nine in the morning or evening. He got up and dressed with haste. He felt strangely buoyant, and had an impulse to jump and sing in a manner unseemly to an elderly scientist. He leapt up the ladder to the control room with no effort at all.

The electric lights were all on and there was no glimmer of daylight.

"That is what I call a good, healthy sleep," Hans Hardt greeted him. "Aren't you lame from lying in bed?"

"I should say not! I feel as fresh and lively as though I had lost ten years while I slept. Has it really been that long?"

Hardt pointed to a clock which showed two thirty in the afternoon.

"Well, I have certainly lost my bearings as to the time. My watch says nine o'clock, your chronometer two-thirty in the afternoon, yet it is still dark."

"Yes, Uncle Alex, according to Friedrichshafen time it is nine o'clock in the morning. You had better set your watch by ship's time now, for it is useless to reckon Our time here according to the local time at some point on the globe. Our time is reckoned from the moment of our departure from the earth."

Anderl was preparing food in the tiny, electrically equipped kitchen. Dr. Hardt paced to and fro with long, elastic strides. He found some difficulty, however, in maintaining his balance.

"When are we going to get some daylight?" he asked.

"As soon as the earth is no longer between us and the sun," was the reply. "That will be at least four hours yet. In the meantime we'll have to be content with the light of the stars and the moon.

Hardt turned out the lights, but the room did not become completely dark. A dim, silvery light penetrated from the outside, casting deep shadows in the cabin. In case of necessity, it would have been quite sufficient for read mg.

"Over there is the moon, but we see only half of it...If it were a full moon, we would have plenty of light. It is not so simple," continued Hardt, "to find one's way through the starry firmament. The constellations which are familiar to us are difficult to distinguish because of the multitude of small, dim stars, invisible from the earth through the naked eye." Pointing through the window he went on: "By looking closely you will be able to recognize the seven stars of the Little Bear, the lowest point of which is the Polar Star, around which, as seen from the earth, the canopy of Heaven seems to turn. For us now it has lost its central position, but it still remains a convenient point from which to determine the direction of the earth's axis, in which it is located, and also the position of the ecliptic."

Anderl appeared with a tray, from which emanated a fragrant aroma of coffee. The three men fell upon the toast and sardines and consumed them with evident relish.

"Shall we throttle some more, Mr. Hardt?" inquired Anderl, taking a huge bite of sandwich between his strong teeth.

"What is our speed now?'

Anderl went over to the switchboard. "A mile and a quarter."

"Let's wait awhile, Anderl, until we have finished our breakfast," replied Hardt with a smile. "Otherwise we'll have indigestion."

"A mile and a quarter a second?" interrupted Dr. Hardt. "Isn't that much slower than we were going right after the start?"

"Yes. At the end of the eighth minute we had reached a parabolic speed of five and a half miles a second, which was to be expected at that altitude. Our speed, of course, does not remain constant, but varies according to the earth's gravitational influence. It is rapid at first, and then gradually diminishes, precisely like that of a stone pitched upward. Before our ship goes down, however, it will reach a point where lunar gravity will prevail. From that point we will travel toward the moon instead of back to the earth. That is the secret of our ability to reach the moon."

"Yes, but why do we no longer have a sense of speed? It seems to me that the *Wieland* has come to a standstill."

"What we felt so sharply at first was the acceleration, not the speed, which, after all, is never perceptible. Have you ever felt aware, in your office at Friedrichshafen, that you were flying through the Universe, without cessation, at the prodigious speed of nearly nineteen miles a second, borne by the earth on her perpetual trip around the sun?"

"Yes, but if the earth, as you say, covers approximately nineteen miles in every second" Dr. Hardt's interest in uranology was momentarily increasing—"there must be something wrong, Hans."

"What?"

"Where could we land with our *Wieland*, making now only a mile and a quarter a second? Won't we, after a few seconds, fall so far behind the speeding earth that there is no possibility of overtaking it?"

"That seems logical at first thought, Uncle Alex, and, according to your theory, conditions are even more to our disadvantage. Not only the earth is dashing away from us, but, as everyone knows, the sun also, with its satellites, is moving toward the constellation of Hercules at a speed of approximately twelve and a half miles a second."

"Great heavens! Then where are we heading for?"

"If we assume, moreover," added Hardt with a quizzical smile, "that the sun revolves around an axis which is also moving, the matter becomes complicated, doesn't it?"

Dr. Hardt was thinking with concentration, but he could find no satisfactory solution of the puzzle.

"Don't worry any more about it, Uncle Alex," said Hardt. "I frankly admit that I myself have no clear idea of absolute speed-if there be such a thing at all. In any event, our ship is proceeding through the Universe, and that's the essential fact."

"You're a queer one, Hans," replied Dr. Hardt. "It certainly is not a matter of indifference to me whether or not we say an eternal farewell to Mother Earth. I have no inclination to sit forever more in your wonderful machine, cruising about in the most remote corners of the Universe."

Hans Hardt was laughing. "Don't worry, Uncle Alex. The earth will not escape us, and let us hope that we, on the other hand, will not escape her. Let me see, how can I reassure you? Our course is exactly determined in the terrestrial solar system, and that is the only thing of importance to us at present. You will understand more clearly, perhaps, with an example."

The engineer reflected for a moment and then continued: "Picture to yourself the dining car of a moving train. An electric fan for ventilation is revolving on the ceiling. On one wing of the fan is perched a small caterpillar. Do you follow me, Uncle Alex?"

"Certainly."

"Good. This caterpillar is creeping from the outer edge of the wing toward the hub—with caterpillar speed, of course. It will reach its goal in a given time, and need feel no concern that it is being carried in a rotary direction by the fan, while at the same time proceeding straight ahead through the progress of the train; more-over, it is being whirled around by the earth in its trip around the sun, and so on. Now can you tell me what is the absolute speed of the caterpillar and in what curve it is proceeding?"

Dr. Hardt scratched his head but found no answer.

"Exactly the same thing applies to the earth," continued Hardt. "The wing of the fan is our earth-moon system. Let us assume that the course of the express train corresponds with the movement of the earth. If the caterpillar wants to leave the fan, say to investigate a bouquet of flowers on a table below, it has to take into ac-count the rotation of the fan. If it wants to escape from the dining car into the open, then it certainly has to govern its actions according to the movement of the train. Likewise in the case of the earth. If we want to travel to Mars, we have to take

By Rocket to the Moon •

the earth's speed into consideration in order to leave the orbit of the earth and enter the path of the neighboring planet. For everything in the world is relative, especially here in the Universe. Do you understand now why I don't know the absolute speed of the *Wieland*, and that possibly there is no such thing?"

How simple it all sounded. And yet it was difficult to detach oneself from the earthly viewpoint and to realize that facts so logical and established as to be taken for granted on earth were fundamentally groundless and even absurd here.

Anderl, too, had been listening with silent interest to these arguments. Now he proceeded to clear the table and carry the dishes into the kitchen.

Dr. Hardt got up. For a long time he looked out the window into the depths of the heavens, and in contemplation of the purity and majesty of the firmament his troubled thoughts dispersed like cosmic dust.

XIV
FAR FROM
THE EARTH'S CONFINES

PRESENTLY something amazing happened. It seemed to Dr. Hardt that he must be dreaming, dreaming the old dream of his childhood that he could fly; that with a few swimming motions of his arms and legs he could rise up above houses and trees and float in sublime freedom over mountains and valleys, an exultant victor over the power of the earth.

Instinctively he drew his knees up to his body and pushed out his legs. His dream was rudely interrupted by a violent blow on his head. He looked dizzily around and discovered that he was moving through the air, gradually sinking toward the floor.

"For Heaven's sake, Hans, where are you?" he called in alarm.

A hearty laugh was the response. "Don't use such Herculean strength in jumping to the ceiling," said Hardt, as he seized his uncle's leg and pulled him to the floor. "Take it easy or you will receive too many bumps."

Once landed safely on the floor, Dr. Hardt crept very cautiously to the wall and held fast to it. "I think I must have been dreaming," he said with uneasiness. His nephew had long before warned him of the approaching moment when terrestrial gravity would cease to be effective, but even so, he was unprepared for this novel experience. Standing at the window, Hans pushed back the gas lever, which almost entirely disconnected the exhaust pipes and greatly reduced the power. To disconnect the pipes altogether was still inadvisable, even for the sake of conserving fuel. Even though the now perceptible pressure was a mere fraction of the earth's gravitational influence, there remained, nevertheless, a minor but quite definite downward pull which gave the space travelers time to prepare themselves for the state of complete independence from the force of gravity. In this state, too, the conception of "above" and "below" was meaningless.

The entire contents of the *Wieland* had now lost the greater part of their weight. The men had become literally as light as feathers, though their muscular strength was unaltered. As a result, each unwary step turned out to be an enormous leap.

Anderl found work in the kitchen entirely pleasant. He could drop plates and cups on any occasion, and they fell so slowly to the floor that nothing broke. With one hand he could easily lift the heavy steel containers in which the fluid oxygen for breathing purposes was kept, though formerly it had been necessary to transport them with jacks and pullies.

When Anderl turned the water faucet, he was confronted with a perplexing problem. The water fell into the basin as usual, but lo and behold! the drops that splashed up kept on ascending into the air and formed a floating, fluid mass which fell gradually to the floor in the form of a puddle.

The occupants of the *Wieland* now experienced an uncomfortable pulling sensation in the chest and in the abdominal region, and also a peculiar quickening of the pulse. On the other hand, they were remarkably insensible to pressure and blows, a condition which was amply demonstrated to them.

Dr. Hardt was studying his body closely, analyzing the effects upon various organs, especially the ears, in an attempt to arrive at the ultimate reason for each symptom. The clearness of his mind and the rapidity with which he drew his conclusions astonished him. As time went on, the symptoms grew less pronounced, and there remained an agreeable freedom from discomfort of any kind, which became evident in the gay and carefree mood of the three lonely men.

The elderly scientist climbed the ladder from the sleeping cabin to the observation cabin with a single bound, while the descent was accomplished in a downward glide through the air. Every unattached article in the ship was floating about, and numerous groans from the vicinity of the ceiling bore witness to the difficulty of learning not to use the muscular strength with which one is endowed by nature. Anderl went about with a broad grin; Dr. Hardt was giggling like a schoolboy; and Hans Hardt's expression was one of utmost good humor.

"I've grown twenty years younger to-day, Hans!" cried Dr. Hardt, as he flapped with ghostlike movements through the air toward his nephew.

"Well, you had better stop there," replied

Hardt with a laugh. "We haven't the proper equipment for nursing babies."

"A trip through the Universe is indeed a wonderful adventure. Later on we will have to build a sanitarium for rejuvenation out here."

"I'm tempted to turn a somersault and slide down the banister," rejoined the engineer gayly, as he pushed himself away from the ceiling where he had kicked himself in a careless moment.

Anderl was singing lustily in the kitchen, something about "What a carefree life we lead," at the same time struggling to no avail with refractory liquids.

Ludicrous events took place at dinner. The soup escaped through the air in a squadron of small fluid balls, until the diners learned to bring the spoon very slowly and carefully to the mouth. An unwitting jar of the table lifted it entirely in to the air, and this sudden ascension of their dinner precipitated a fantastic whirl of men and chairs hurtling about the room. In the midst of the general commotion, Hardt's little canary, chirping in alarm, fluttered around the light, supporting its cage on its wings.

"How much do I weigh now?" cried Dr. Hardt through the hubbub.

Hans tried to suppress his uncontrollable gayety, which was scarcely befitting the dignity of the captain of a spaceship. "We have now only ten centimeters of acceleration pressure, which approximates one hundredth of the normal gravitational pressure. Anything which weighs one hundred pounds on earth is here reduced to about one pound. Therefore, your weight would amount to no more than a good pound, Uncle Alex."

To prevent further damage, Anderl screwed the furniture to the floor. The little yellow bird, too, was denied its privilege of flight by its cage being made fast. At last peace and quiet were restored to the *Wieland.*

Since the spaceship was now proceeding on its own momentum along its cosmic course, and needed no further guiding, Hans and his uncle sat down for a chat. They fastened themselves to their chairs with leather straps, without which they could not have remained in their seats. The slightest movement would have wafted them upward like feathers.

Outside was the darkness of a starry night.

The position of the earth was discernible only as a dark, empty space, which had the appearance of an enormous abyss in the midst of the firmament below.

Dr. Hardt broke the silence. "Hans, there is something that puzzles me."

"That is not surprising, Uncle Alex," replied Hardt. "For me, too, strange events have occurred."

"I am referring to this decrease in weight. When I, as you say, weigh no more than a pound, it still does not follow that I should hover are like some little angel. A pound is a weight which normally drops quickly to the floor."

"You are touching there a subject very difficult to explain. You know that weight is more than impeded movement and that the earth attracts all bodies. A stone lying on the ground cannot follow this attraction. Therefore pressure which it exerts on the place beneath has a weight corresponding to its acceleration, were there nothing to prevent its falling. This acceleration is on the same scale for all bodies on the surface of the earth. A stone dropped from a church tower falls five meters in the first second, fifteen meters in the next, twenty-five meter in the third, and so on. Its acceleration increases by ten meters in each second, or, more exactly, 9.80 meters. You will, perhaps, remember this figure, 9.80, was indicated in school by letter G as the normal acceleration of the earth. Thus the stone drops, in all, forty-five meters in the first three seconds. Now if bodies in our *Wieland* have but one-hundredth of their normal weight, they fall, instead of forty-five meters in the first three seconds, only that many centimeters. Inasmuch as their weight has vanished, their descent is very gradual."

"I understand perfectly. And this decrease in weight is due to the earth's greatly diminished magnetism at such a distance?"

"That conclusion is nearly, though not exactly, correct. For the rest, our weight is dependent on the activity of our exhaust pipes."

Dr. Hardt looked up in astonishment. "Do you mean to tell me that our weight varies according to your manipulation of the fuel-control lever?"

"That is precisely what I mean," calmly replied Hardt.

"But, my dear man, you must realize that even with your remarkable machine you can't turn off gravity according to your fancy—or can you?"

"Of course I am unable to do that," said the engineer with a smile. "The earth's attraction remains effective, though to a very slight degree, at this distance."

"Well, then, I'd like to know how you are going to get yourself out of this predicament," said Dr. Hardt, doubtfully shaking his head.

"See here, Uncle Alex. If I disconnect the pipes entirely, the ship with all its contents will oppose no resistance to gravitation. It will become like a falling stone, which, with nothing to hold it up, is weightless. The contents of the interior will have no more pressure than a knapsack on the back of a man falling from a precipice."

"Nice prospects we have, then, of landing with a crash on Lake Constance when we go back."

"No, there is no danger of that, because of the high rate of acceleration which we made such a struggle to attain during our ascent. We are describing a true gravitational curve in the form of a parabola, or better, hyperbola, directed toward the infinite. We are, in fact, falling, not with increasing speed downward but with decreasing speed upward."

"Falling upward!" exclaimed Dr. Hardt. "How can that be, Hans? Really, the hieroglyphics of Peruvian Maya are simple in comparison with these mathematical problems of yours."

In his perturbation, Dr. Hardt gesticulated rather wildly. The straps confining him to the chair worked loose, and he turned a perfect somersault into the air. Hans assisted the mortified doctor to regain his lost dignity and resumed the conversation.

"No, no, Uncle Alex! Everybody understands best whatever he has especially studied. Your researches in regard to the primeval age and your interpretations of legends are to me as incomprehensible as would be to Anderl a law forbidding him to drink beer. In any event, one fact remains, Uncle Alex: We shall be weightless whenever the natural movement of our *Wieland*, which is caused by gravitation, is wholly independent of extraneous influences, such as mechanical force from within, or air resistance from without, irrespective of proximity to the earth or to some other planet."

XV
THE STOWAWAY

THE discussion between Hardt and his uncle was interrupted at this juncture by a violent uproar from the direction of the supply room. Angry vociferations from Anderl betokened utmost exasperation over some cause not yet apparent to the listeners.

"Just wait, you good-for-nothing scoundrel!

I'll help you out of there, thief!"

An unwelcome suspicion suddenly occurred to Hardt.

"Anderl, what's the matter down there?" he called.

Anderl, unheeding, continued to berate the unseen culprit in strident tones. "Traitor! Listen to me! If you don't come out of there this minute, I'll knock you in the jaw so hard that you'll have to be carried out on a stretcher. Well, how about it?"

A fearful din ensued. Cases crashed, cans clattered, boxes rattled.

"There, you rat, I've got you!" came from Anderl. Presently he appeared in the control room, dragging after him a struggling figure, whose efforts to escape sent them both whirling about in the air in a confused tangle of madly waving arms and legs. Hans grasped one of the legs, pulled the two combatants to the floor and separated them.

"Say, Anderl's a roughneck, and that's no joke!" exclaimed the newcomer. Hardt, to his extreme discomfiture, recognized-Tommy Bighead.

"Where have you been hiding?" demanded Hardt.

"He hid himself in the supply room," said Anderl before Tommy had a chance to reply. "He got hungry and came out. The contemptible wretch grabbed half a ham, and a four-pound piece of pork. I just happened to see him as he was sneaking out of the kitchen into his hiding place behind the tool boxes. He wouldn't come out until I coaxed him a little."

Hardt had heard the "coaxing."

"Be quiet, Anderl," he commanded, as he looked inquiringly at their uninvited guest. Tommy was a sight to behold. He was bruised and bleeding from his scuffle with Anderl. He had had no elastic hammock to protect him during the ascent, moreover, and the intense pressure must have left him in bad condition.

"How did you manage to slip into the ship before our departure?" questioned the engineer.

"Oh, that was easy," replied Tommy. "I got hold of a key to the supply room, and while you were showing the reporters around the *Wieland*, I went in there and made myself comfortable."

"Mr. Bighead," thundered Hardt, "you have committed an unprecedented breach of faith. This adventure may be fatal for you. Do you realize that I hold in my power the life of each passenger in my ship?"

"No. I am a citizen of the United States of America, and the best reporter in the State of Michigan. If you bump me off, you will break the contract. I'm the only one who has the right and duty to publish articles on the trip to the moon. Can a dead man write articles?"

Hardt hesitated between amusement and anger at the daring impudence of the reporter.

"In order to write decent articles," continued Tommy, "I had to go along on the trip. I told you that in Friedrichshafen. Well, Tommy Bighead is keeping his word!"

The engineer paced up and down the cabin.

Presently he paused in front of Tommy and said in a stinging tone: "Excuse your action on anyway, we might just as well take a look at the moon first. Only it is too bad-is there any possible way of communicating with the earth? It would be a shame for Mr. Tiller not to receive a report for the Michigan Evening Post. He would hold it against me if I were in my grave and would sue my heirs for the unrecovered two hundred thousand dollars."

In spite of his anger, Hardt had to admit admiration for Tommy's fearlessness. Here was no weakling in the face of death. In a predicament, where the average person would think only of his own safety, Tommy's chief concern was to fulfill his duty toward his paper. Though Hardt had frequently smiled at the presumptuous title of "best reporter in the State of Michigan," he was now willing to grant that Tommy really deserved such a title. His tone was considerably milder when he directed Tommy to take a much needed rest, after which they would discuss the somewhat changed aspect of their journey.

Tommy obeyed with reluctance. On passing Anderl, he allowed plenty of space between, and then he disappeared into the sleeping quarters below.

"That fellow is impudent," commented Dr.

Hardt. "You were too easy with him, Hans."

"That's right, Dr. Hardt," confirmed Anderl in a tone of fury. "A good beating up is what he needs to teach him not to steal hams!"

"What's the use of that!" said Hardt impatiently. "You forget he raised the money for us. But he's here now and we can't put him out. The important thing is to work out this fuel problem."

"Does a fourth man really make the landing dangerous?" inquired Dr. Hardt.

"Unfortunately, he does," was the reply. "Shortly before we start maneuvering to land, we have to throw overboard anything that is superfluous weight, like tools, food supplies, kitchen furniture, and even the optical instruments. All the things that were necessary to us during the trip will have to be sacrificed before our final landing, or else our fuel will not be sufficient to prevent a crash. It will not be easy to find the equivalent of the reporter's weight to throw out. There is no denying Tommy Bighead has played us a mean trick."

Whereupon Hardt fell into a serious meditation, while his companions maintained complete silence..

XVI
SUNRISE IN THE UNIVERSE

THE ensuing half hour passed by without event. There was nothing to be seen outside the spaceship, save a multitude of brilliant stars on the nocturnal firmament and the pale disc of the moon which seemed to occupy a stationary position far down toward the equator. Dr. Hardt had wondered, at first, why the course of the *Wieland* was not directed toward the moon. With his newly acquired astronomical knowledge, however, he was able to calculate precisely how fast the moon was moving in its orbit around the earth. His conclusion was that, whereas the moon had not yet reached the point toward which they were heading, it would reach that point in advance of the spaceship.

A cry from Anderl aroused Dr. Hardt from his meditations. "See that bow of fire down there! That's the earth!"

The three travelers quickly gathered around the window to gaze into the abyss of the Universe. Far below, around the right outer edge of the black, starless space which indicated the location of the earth, blazed a vast, fiery crescent. The sun's rays from the rim of the earth were radiating an aureole of shimmering flame. Against this multi-colored background arose the dark, arched silhouette of the terrestrial planet. It seemed as if the mighty disc, which at this distance appeared in its relatively much larger dimensions than the moon, had burst into flame and was emitting great waves of energy. The delicate crescent of the moon, almost invisible, hovered on its side as though shrinking from the earth's overwhelming arch of light.

The occupants of the *Wieland* watched, in awe, this magnificent spectacle, which would leave an indelible impression with the most callous observer.

"No human being has ever seen that before!" whispered Dr. Hardt. "Sunrise in the Universe! It must be a dream!"

"Anderl, call Mr. Bighead," commanded Hardt.

His uncle gave a nod of agreement. It would have been a pity to leave the reporter sleeping through this phenomenon of unforgettable grandeur.

At that moment the American appeared.

"What's up?" he asked. Then, glancing through the window, he, too, fell into amazed silence.

The splendor of the vision increased. The rays of light seemed to concentrate into a blinding point at the crown of the arch; then, slowly, the sun appeared above the black rim of the earth. It was impossible to watch the dazzling light without sunglasses.

"Look! Day is breaking!" came from the commander.

Upon directing their attention to the spaceship, the watchers discovered that it was daylight. The sunlight was penetrating the ship from below, and cast a dazzling reflection on the curved deck. The hammocks across the windows were like transparent curtains. After eighteen hours of traveling through darkness, the *Wieland* was to continue her journey through brilliant daylight.

Although a bright, warm flood of sunshine penetrated the part of the ship turned toward the sun, the opposite side faced heavy darkness. While golden and cloudless day smiled through the windows of the one side, black night yawned through the windows of the other side.

This was not like day on earth. The *Wieland* was not spanned by blue sky, but surrounded by a dark firmament with tranquilly shining stars.

By protecting the eyes with the hand from the glowing white disc, one could distinguish even the stars in close proximity to the sun. Copernicus, with such a ship at his disposal, could have seen the planet Mercury before going to his grave.

The parts of the ship touched directly by the sun's rays, such as the outer window frames, shone with a supernatural, phosphorescent luster, standing out in bold relief against the dark sky and reflecting light into the interior.

The *Wieland* had finally passed beyond the last vestige of the earth's influence. Irresistibly drawn on its solitary cosmic path, its distance from the earth hourly increased by thousands of miles.

The increasing light from the earth brought into visibility the spherical outline of the planet toward which they were traveling. At various intervals the exact distance between the spaceship and the earth could easily be calculated and their speed reckoned. Since there were no clouds to obstruct the view, the brownish contours of the earth were distinguishable on its illuminated side, which was sharply outlined against the dark background of the sea. North of the Tropic of Cancer the dull brown of the continental masses turned into a light gray, for the northern hemisphere was covered with winter snow. The North Pole was concealed by the obscurity of the Polar night.

Dr. Hardt sat for hours looking through the telescope, which was now pointed downward. He watched different sections of the earth emerge from the darkness, glide across the bright disc, and disappear on the outer edge. The rotation of the earth, too, could be observed, in the same manner as the movements of the sinking moon can be followed from the earth. The areas of large cities appeared like dim, yet visible dots. The shadows of great mountain ranges, like the Cordilleras, the Alps, the Carpathians and the Himalayas facilitated the identification of the various countries.

"Wouldn't it be fine," suddenly remarked Dr. Hardt, "if we had a telescope powerful enough to distinguish buildings. In that case we could look right down into Friedrichshafen and guide the course of the airships. It would be like acting the part of Divine Providence. A turn of the screw, and the eye would travel from Bucharest to New York."

"Have patience, Uncle Alex, and you will have such a telescope at your command," replied Hardt, beating his arms about as though chilled. "After we have finished our trip in the *Wieland*, I will build on its exterior a combination of lenses which will surpass in effectiveness the greatest telescopes in the world. There is no turbid, light-absorbing air here to prevent us from using very strong magnifiers. By the way, don't you find that it is becoming extremely cold?"

As a matter of fact, the temperature in the ship was below freezing. The heat derived from air surrounding the earth had long since vanished, and the electric system was no longer able to counteract the increasing cold.

"There is a simple means of securing the desired temperature," said Hardt. "I need only utilize the warmth of the sun, but..."

"What do you mean by 'but'?" exclaimed Dr.

Hardt. "It surely won't do any harm to use a little of the sun's abundant heat."

"Certainly not to the sun, but what about Mr. Kamphenkel?"

"Good heavens, Hans, are you crazy? What has Kamphenkel to do with the fact that we are freezing up here?"

"He has to have the assurance that the *Wieland* is still in existence."

"And how is that?"

"Well, you noticed before we started that the exterior of our ship was black on one side but had a highly polished, reflecting surface on the other side. As long as the reflecting side of the *Wieland* is turned toward the sun, we are visible from the earth. Unfortunately, however, not only the sunlight is then reflected earthward, but also heat. By turning the black side toward the sun, the rays are absorbed and the heat penetrates the interior instead of radiating into space. Under those conditions we would be warm in the ship, but the people on earth would be wondering what had become of the *Wieland*. The small amount of light reflected by the black surface would not be sufficient to penetrate the air enveloping the earth. After all, we are 93,750 miles distant from the earth."

"That wouldn't do," declared the scientist. "Couldn't we solve the difficulty by increasing the ship's artificial heat?"

"To change a temperature of 454 degrees below zero to a comfortable temperature would be impossible with the artificial means at our disposal. We'll just have to put that idea out of our heads. Our only recourse is temporarily to disappear from the sight of observers on earth."

"How can the ship be turned over?"

"There are three huge flywheels between our living quarters and the tanks. These are run by small electromotors. Their axes are perpendicular to each other and move in a clockwise fashion when set in motion. According to the law of reaction, the rotation of the flywheel whose axis runs parallel to the lengthwise axis of the ship causes the ship to roll in the opposite direction. The ship can thus be placed in any desired position by connecting the proper flywheel. Great speed in the rotation of these wheels is, of course, necessary. If the ship is to make a complete revolution in one minute, the flywheel must rotate at a much higher rate of speed, in view of its small size as compared with the size of the ship."

With this explanation, Hardt connected a motor. There became audible a dull droning noise, which increased until it became a loud whistling sound. Slowly and almost imperceptibly the sun and the earth seemed to circle around the ship. The revolution was completed in half a minute, after which the whistling changed into a buzz and whir, and finally died out. Just as before, the sunlight penetrated obliquely through the windows from below, only now from the opposite side. If unaware of what had been taking place, no one would have noticed any change.

This was the moment when the people on earth were thrown into a panic of anxiety, believing that Hardt's spaceship was lost.

XVII
PERFECT FREEDOM

A S the action of the exhaust pipes gradually died down, the movements of the space travelers became more and more problematical. They could no longer walk about in a normal manner. Every unpremeditated motion resulted in a glide in an unexpected direction or a sudden somersault through the middle of the room. Only through slow, careful creeping was it possible to progress to a desired point. Handgrips conveniently placed at frequent intervals enabled the travelers to cling to the floor, wall or ceiling.

Gravity had only one thousandth of its original attraction, and the weight of a man had, in consequence, diminished to about seventy grams. Hans Hardt now invited his uncle to take his first flight from the ship—a flight in the true sense of the word. Dr. Hardt was at first reluctant to leave the *Wieland*'s shelter and confide himself to the tender mercies of empty space. The novelty of the adventure lured, however, and his curiosity got the better of his concern, for safety. By this time, moreover, he was so accustomed to weightlessness that he was proof against surprises on that score.

The pneumatic outfits lay ready in the pilot's cabin. Hans Hardt had already donned his, and was carefully inspecting the helmet before putting it on.

"The pressure is now so slight," he reassured his still wavering uncle, "that once outside, an acceleration of only a centimeter a second will enable us to keep up with the ship. That eliminates all possibility of danger."

"Is that so!" answered Dr. Hardt. "Do you know, I am finally becoming accustomed to the idea that, instead of hanging by a hair, our life is dependent upon your mathematical formulas. Death would be merely a slight mistake in arithmetic."

"Is that so far from the case on earth?" replied Hardt with a laugh.

He then proceeded to give a few more directions and admonitions to return immediately to the ship in case of any difficulty in breathing. He instructed his uncle in the use of the telephone cable wound around a spool and attached to his suit at the chest. One end of the cable entered the helmet, where it connected with a microphone. The other end was to be attached to one of the numerous switch boxes fastened to the outside of the ship's hull.

"Do not forget," he concluded, "to connect the cable immediately. We can then speak with each other and remain in communication with Anderl, as well as pull ourselves back to the ship by the cable. All right, let's go!"

Hardt impressed upon Anderl the importance of not altering the action of the exhaust pipes. After finally convincing himself that the helmets were correctly adjusted, he opened the inner door of the vaulted cabin, allowed Dr. Hardt to enter, then carefully closed the door and turned a valve to let the air escape from the cabin. The rubber outfits were inflated to such an extent that the small space was hardly sufficient to contain them. The engineer opened the outer door and the two men glided out into space.

Dr. Hardt crept cautiously along the smooth hull of the ship and looked for a switchbox. Immediately upon connecting the cable, he heard Hans's voice as though from a great distance, whereas his companion was in reality no more than a few feet away.

"Uncle Alex," said the voice, "do you understand me? Are you breathing all right?"

Perfectly," was the reply. The communication was satisfactorily established.

The two figures joined their leather-covered hands and began to move around the *Wieland*, while the cables unwound from the spools. Had they not already been accustomed to the lack of gravity, the first unwary motion would have sent them far from the ship. As it was, they found difficulty in keeping close to it.

"What is that?" called out Dr. Hardt in alarm.

"What has happened to the ship?" He pointed in the direction of the exhaust pipes. The rapid movement had upset his balance, and he was gradually withdrawing from the ship and floating out into space.

"What could have happened?" replied Hans Hardt, who, likewise, was no longer able to hold on and was drifting away.

"Look at our proud *Wieland*," said Dr. Hardt.

In his eagerness, he did not notice that he was really flying. "She looks as if she had the measles."

As a matter of fact, the rear of the ship was covered with vari-colored spots of different sizes, glittering in the sun. Hardt laughed. Through the telephone it sounded like a cough.

"Don't worry, Uncle Alex! Those spots are merely flecks of ice being melted by the sun. The vapor, which adhered to the ship during its ascent, later froze."

The cables had, in a short time, unwound to their full length, and the two men, like captive balloons, hovered at a distance of three hundred and twenty-five feet. Although their helmets glistened brightly, their suits remained in complete darkness. Day and night had come into a seemingly impossible conjunction.

The spaceship sped through the Universe like a gigantic torpedo, a strange glittering monster trailing behind it a gleaming white veil of mist.

"How are we going to get back again?" asked Dr. Hardt, when the measle spots had ceased to worry him.

"In the pocket of your suit you will find a small repeating pistol," came the reply. "Shoot it off once, and the kick of the pistol will set you into motion. You can then pull yourself back with the cable."

Dr. Hardt followed these directions, and anon he had safely regained the ship. Reassured by the effectiveness of the shot, he began to prowl around the *Wieland*. A feeling of unrestrained freedom and merriment permeated his whole being, and he could have shouted with joy, despite his fifty-four years of earthly existence. It was pleasant to float thus without effort through the brilliancy of the sunlight against the dark background of the starry heavens.

There was no more "up" and "down." Only a gentle pull in the direction of the exhaust pipes reminded one of the fact that there was still a "below." That was not for long, however. Hardt had given instructions for a complete disconnection of the exhaust pipes for the next half hour. During that period was to disappear the last trace of pressure reminding one of earthly connections.

"Be careful, Uncle Alex!" exclaimed the engineer suddenly. "Beware of the exhaust pipes! Even though the cable won't reach the stern of the ship, it is possible for it to break. If you get near the gas exhaust in your pneumatic suit, it won't be a mistake in arithmetic that sends you to eternity."

"I'll be careful," replied Dr. Hardt, turning quickly about. He was a trifle frightened at not seeing the speaker, and he had forgotten about the telephone.

The entrance into the ship was made in the same manner as the exit. On reaching the outer cabin, Hans Hardt opened a valve which admitted air from the interior of the ship until the pressure was equal on both sides of the inner door. The door was then easily opened, and the fliers could lay aside their pneumatic suits and relate their experiences to each other without the use of a telephone.

"It is incredible!" exclaimed Dr. Hardt, still dazed by his adventure. "It wasn't the least bit cold out there!"

"The air strata in the inflated suit, with the hard exterior, protected us in the same manner as a thermos bottle protects from loss of heat," explained Hardt. "As long as the suits are airtight, there is not the least danger. Incidentally, did you notice that our spaceship was proceeding at the rate of fifty miles a minute?"

"No!" answered Dr. Hardt in amazement. "It seemed as if we were in some kind of cosmic health resort instead of on a journey."

"It is the same old story of the caterpillar and the windmill. In our case the *Wieland* is standing still, while the earth is moving away from us and the moon is coming toward us. That is true, however, only so long as the movement of our ship is not essentially influenced. It is best not to think about it at all."

Anderl was allowed to go out next, after being instructed as to the use of the handgrips and how to move while crawling about. Tommy Bighead, too, received a suit.

The next thing on the program was the construction of the great telescope already discussed. A shaded, concave mirror of silver leaf, several yards long, was projected about three hundred and twenty-five feet from the ship on long, metal supports. The reflections on the mirror converged through a lens to the telescope stationed in the control room. By means of a cord, the mirror could be shifted in any direction from the lens, and the desired locality could be covered.

It afforded an indescribable pleasure to explore the earth through this simple telescope, searching out each contour of the mainland in its many-thousandfold enlargement. Even the more prominent structures of large cities were distinguishable. The rotation of the earth, however, carried the focused points so quickly out of the field of vision that a great deal of practice was necessary to be able to follow the movement with the aid of the primitive controlling cord.

In the meantime, Hardt had totally disconnected the exhaust pipes, and the last faint trace of gravity had disappeared. There was no longer any "above" or "below." Anything not screwed down floated freely about through the rooms. Where there were no handgrips to aid them, the men used swimming motions with their arms and legs for circulating through the interior. The idea of lying on a bed was absurd. Indeed, it would have required a great effort to keep from falling off. One slept while wafted gently about the room; Dr. Hardt smoked his pipe in a luxurious armchair of space; and the little canary, with useless wings, huddled silently in its cage, a bewildered spectator of this enchanted world.

Chairs and tables were stowed away in the supply room;

hammocks were rolled up; and the rope ladders removed for lack of utility. Under such conditions the human being had no need of other comfort than free and empty space.

Anderl, in the kitchen, was in steady combat with obstinate liquids. The only possible way to empty a bottle was to draw out the contents with a straw. If it so happened that a bottle was thoughtlessly left uncorked, the contents flowed out and floated around the room in drops which were not easy to recapture.

The space travelers had soon accustomed themselves to passing most of their time outside of the ship. Only the limited capacity of the oxygen containers and the necessity of eating and sleeping prevented them from taking up their permanent quarters outside. Whoever was not on duty in the ship climbed out onto the exterior of the *Wieland* and circulated about through the ether, more lightly than a bird on wing.

Passing the time thus pleasantly, they did not notice that the moon which, in the meantime, had become almost three-quarters full, was rising higher and higher above the ship until it leaned sidewise over the control in a threatening manner. It was the third day of their journey, and the ship had reached the region of space where the diminishing attraction of the earth just balanced that of the moon. Once beyond this boundary line of gravity, the *Wieland* was no longer subject to terrestrial influence. She had entered the realm of the moon, and was descending with increasing speed to the lunar masses, whose disc greatly surpassed the earth in apparent magnitude.

From this time on, Hardt prohibited everyone from leaving the ship.

XVIII
AN UNEXPECTED DISCOVERY

THE nearer the *Wieland* came to its goal, the more uneasy became Tommy Bighead. Time after time he asked the commander of the ship if there were any possibility of transmitting news to the earth. He had written an accurate report of all the notable phenomena and occurrences of this adventurous trip, and it troubled him not to be able to communicate this highly interesting and valuable news to Mr. Tiller.

"It is impossible, Mr. Bighead!" emphatically declared Hardt for the hundredth time. "There are no implements in existence by which we could send messages over 187,500 miles. Besides, we have no transmitter, and if we did have one, it would be useless."

"How about light signals?" inquired Tommy eagerly.

"That is conceivable, with the aid of a large, flat mirror. But the prospect of such signals being perceived is extremely slight. Besides, Central Europe lies under dense skies."

"Nevertheless," persisted Tommy, "at least one of the numerous astronomical observatories on earth will have an unobstructed view. Something will penetrate through the density. Suppose we just flash, up, or down, or over, to the earth. Someone will notice us."

Hardt smiled. "My dear Mr. Bighead," he said, "how do you figure that out? Do you think we can experiment over 187,500 miles as though it were an artillery maneuver field? Our flashes would be discernible from the earth only by means of the most modern refractors with powerful magnifiers. Even with such instruments, a high brilliancy of light would be necessary, and the instruments pointed exactly in our direction. In addition to that, our reflecting mirror would have to be directed approximately toward the observatory watching us. We cannot transmit to the observatories, hoping that at that precise moment a telescope is focused on us, with an observer at the eyepiece who is sufficiently keen to interpret our flashes as the Morse code, besides being able to read that code. You rely to greatly on the blind chance, Mr. Bighead."

"It certainly is too bad that my sensational news can't be published," lamented Tommy. "It will have to remain unpublished until we return-if we do return," was the reply.

There it was again, that continual reproach which was driving Tommy to the point of distraction. In every glance and gesture, Tommy felt Hardt's silent accusation, "You have our lives on your conscience!" Each hour of the journey increased Tommy's torment, at the same time bringing nearer the unsuccessful termination of the adventure, which would be attributable to him. His impenetrable mask of indifference fell aside at last, revealing the distorted countenance of one tormented by bitter remorse and anxiety.

In order to find temporary relief from his very unhappy thoughts, Tommy became deeply engrossed in studying the parts of the moon which took shape in the brilliant light, constantly increasing in size as the distance grew less. Deserts and plains, grooved with deep furrows, alternated with dark, round craters and jagged mountains which cast long shadows. No forest, river or sea relieved the grim desolation. From northern to southern extremity, as far as the sun spread its revealing light, only bare, uncultivated land and rugged mountain ranges appeared. There was no sign of plant life. The view of the old satellite's wrinkled and shrunken features was unimpeded by cloud or atmosphere.

On the northwestern section of the moon was the large, circular mountain range called Copernicus, comprising several concentric mountain ranges which inclosed a broad, kettle-like depression. The area surrounding this depression disclosed many black fissures. The barren summits of the imposing mass rose more than 13,000 feet above the moon's level, and threw deep black shadows over the neighboring ranges.

A darker point, apparently inside the broad crater, aroused Tommy's curiosity. Was he deceiving himself, or was the point really moving? Now it had reached the edge of the crater and was creeping across the mountain range. What could it be? Could there be life and movement on this dead, desolate moon? He promptly informed Hans Hardt of his discovery and the latter focused the telescope upon it.

"Indeed," he said with much interest, "you are right. The point is moving, and it is moving fast. Take a look at the time."

"Twenty minutes and eight seconds after four."

"Thank you. Please tell me when exactly two minutes have elapsed."

Hardt did not allow the mysterious point to leave his vision. On the telescope's scale he read the exact angle around which the point had moved during the two minutes. Knowing the distance to the moon, he could reckon the distance covered by the point.

"In the two minutes, this object has covered about 105 miles," he said enthusiastically, when he had finished his calculations. "It must, therefore, have a speed of nearly a mile a second. That is more than the speed of our *Wieland*."

"What do you make of it?" inquired Dr. Hardt anxiously.

"That it cannot be a point on the moon, but a body hovering in space between us and the moon."

"Is it a second spaceship, then?"

Hardt shook his head, laughing. "I can, under no consideration, believe that is true. The *Wieland* is the first ship carrying men to leave the earth."

"Are you quite sure of that, Hans?" countered the scientist. "Of course, there has been no mention of a cruise through the Universe in all history, nor of even an attempt to make such a cruise. The brief span of time, however, bearing the proud name of 'history,' is only an episode in the life of this planet. Do we know what happened three thousand years ago? Do we know whether or not a highly developed human race once inhabited the earth, whose knowledge and power surpassed our much renowned age of scientific achievement, and which probably became extinct in some former cataclysm? Finally, is it not curious that the myths and fables of all earthly inhabitants mention only one great destroying flood, the Deluge?"

"Your imagination certainly is working, Uncle Alex!" laughed Hardt. "I was thinking that this is a minute terrestrial body revolving about the moon as a satellite, just as the moon itself revolves about the earth and the earth the sun. Thanks to its small size, no astronomer on the earth has become aware of its existence. Look! The point has just reached the edge of the moon. In a moment it will be beyond it."

After a quarter of an hour the body in question hovered to the side of the moon at a distance of a quarter of the moon's diameter.

"Now it appears to have gone as far from the side as it can," announced Hardt, looking through the telescope. "Correct. It is slowly approaching the moon again and will soon disappear behind it."

Hardt now proceeded to calculate the approximate course of the tiny satellite. "To make a complete revolution, the body requires three hours. It revolves around the moon at a distance of 481 miles."

Dr. Hardt was seized with a reawakened desire for exploration. "Hans, since we did not contemplate landing on the moon during this first trip, what do you think—" He hesitated, but went on quickly. "It would be a shame not to bring home any positive report. Couldn't we at least find out the secret of this little star?"

The engineer pondered for some time before answering. "It is not entirely impossible."

He then unfolded the following plan to his enthralled companions. "First, the speed of the *Wieland* must be increased to that of the satellite. This is already taking place while our rocket is being drawn to the moon in a prescribed course. At present it is describing the arch of Kepler's narrow gravitational parabola, in whose focus stands the center of the moon, and which is leading us constantly nearer the moon's surface. At the same time, our speed is steadily increasing in an unimpeded fall!."

"When the distance of the satellite from the moon measures a little less than 500 miles, it describes a circular course with a 1,562-mile radius around the moon. Is it possible to cause the *Wieland* to gravitate in a similar course around the moon?"

"Exactly that! Even though we would then have the same speed as the satellite, we could not overtake it. I deem it safer to approach as near to the moon as possible to gain a really high speed."

"And then?"

"Then we will glide at a tangent over the surface of the moon and leave it again, arriving behind the moon on the path of the satellite. At that point we shall have a speed greater · than that of our goal, and it can be throttled down as the occasion requires. It will, of course, not be easy to adapt the speed of the *Wieland* to that of the satellite, and an absolute equality of speeds is necessary to make the connection. Nevertheless, the attempt would be interesting as an experiment, and we might be rewarded by a visit to this satellite."

"Let's go!" eagerly exclaimed Anderl. "Let's go exploring! What a lark!"

Hardt shook his head. "If chance doesn't aid us, then we can't bring it about by force. We can encircle the moon as often as we wish. It costs no power—a few shots at the most—to establish our direction, which is a minor consideration. Unfortunately, though, we are not in a position to overtake the satellite, as that would tax our fuel supply too greatly."

"That's a shame!" commented Dr. Hardt with an air of resignation.

Anderl raged at the American who was responsible for this hindrance to their plans.

Tommy himself had turned ghastly pale and silently withdrew. He could no longer endure these reproaches. His excess of enthusiasm was ending in a grim decision-vague and undefined at first, but gradually taking definite form.

"Hang it all!" said he to himself. "You've made your bed, Tommy, and now you can lie in .it."

From that time on he moved like a sleepwalker.

XIX
TOMMY MAKES
HIS EXIT

THERE shortly arrived a very moment for Tommy to carry out his desperate plan. Hardt and Anderl were creeping about the ship's lower cabins, for the purpose of inspecting and making ready for use the available parts of the rocket. Close proximity to the moon necessitated utmost caution, for the slightest defect in current regulator, fly wheel, or any other part of the complicated mechanism, would jeopardize the lives of the space travelers.

Dr. Hardt was sitting at the telescope, observing with scientific thoroughness the interior of the large crater where he had notice what he thought to be a whitish vapor. He had neither eye nor ear for his immediate surroundings, and Tommy could proceed unmolested with the accomplishment of his purpose.

Anyone but Tommy would have merely jumped out of the ship to immediate annihilation. In space without air and pressure, any human organism would have to collapse from inward pressure. Not so, however, with practical and business-like Tommy. He had no intention of throwing away his life so cheaply. "If I am to reach a sudden collapse," thought he to himself, "the experience must be accompanied by an entirely novel sensation. Before that happens, I should like to experience as many other sensations as possible."

Possibly Tommy cherished the secret hope that the others, upon their return to earth, would describe his death in detail, thus establishing his eternal fame as a reporter.

His escape was carefully planned. After eating a huge meal,

his last, he donned the rubberized suit and placed on his back three oxygen tanks, each containing a six-hour supply of oxygen. "Eighteen hours is a long time," he thought. "Anything might happen in that time!" He filled all his pockets with cartridges for the pistol, and tied a bag of additional ammunition around his waist. Finally he wrote a few words on a slip of paper which he attached to the hook where his pneumatic suit usually hung. And now, with his helmet firmly screwed on, he cautiously opened the door to the vault and made his exit into space.

For a time, Tommy lingered near the ship in shuddering contemplation of the rapidly approaching moon, which, by this time, nearly blotted out the view of the firmament. Had not the perception of "above" and "below" vanished with the loss of gravity, Tommy would have had the impression that the *Wieland* was falling obliquely to the mainland from a great height. The longer he gazed at the glittering, jagged mountain peaks, the greater became his disinclination to carry out his scheme. He was tempted to turn back and regain the protecting shelter of the ship. There was still time. On thinking of his late companions, however, and of their pitiless reproaches, he regretted his cowardice.

"Go on, Tommy," he said to himself, clenching his teeth. Mustering all his strength, he drew up his knees and made a mighty leap out into the gloom. The speed thus created carried him steadily away from the ship. On looking back, he saw the great hull of the *Wieland* gleaming brightly against the darkness beyond. It all seemed like a nightmare.

Tommy drew out his pistol and aimed it at the ship as though leading an attack against it. As he was aware, however, it contained only blank cartridges. Four times he fired. He saw the flash of fire at the muzzle but heard no explosion. These repeated shots lent considerable speed to his solitary departure from the ship, which grew smaller in the distance until it was a mere flicker of light in the broad expanse of space.

And so, Tommy proceeded through the abyss of the Universe, a free, isolated earthly body. The hours passed. The *Wieland* had vanished. Unbroken silence enveloped the forlorn figure. It was only the shifting location of the moon mountains which enabled him to realize that he was not hovering, motionless, in space, but falling obliquely toward the giant disc. His solitude became unbearable. The dismal silence oppressed his ears like the roar of Niagara Falls back home. Should he bring it all to a sudden end? He was tortured by his indecision as to whether he should rip open his protecting outfit or gradually go insane in this hideous isolation. The possibility of rescue kept recurring to him. Should he go back to the *Wieland*? No! Anyway, he had lost his sense of direction and had no idea as to how to reach the ship.

Two possibilities lay before him: the curved path of his flight would either follow a revolving course around the moon, in which case, he could live for fifteen hours, as long as his supply of oxygen held out, and then suffocate; or, his journey would terminate somewhere on the moon's surface, within two hours at the most, and the impact of his landing would crush him into atoms. In either case he was irrevocably lost! A third possibility did not occur to him.

Tommy groaned. He began to talk to himself for the sake of hearing a human voice, and was shocked at the dull, croaking sound within his helmet. The cold crept over his limbs. In the course of time, even the air-space of his suit could not protect his body from loss of heat, and he shivered with the increasing chill. He moved his legs and arms rapidly about in a vain effort to warm himself. What was the use? It would soon be over, anyway. And he resigned himself to his inevitable fate.

For a while Tommy could feel an agitated palpitation of his heart. His senses became numbed. Only his brain continued to work with astonishing precision. Long-forgotten incidents recurred to him. The events of his past flashed through his mind in kaleidoscopic clarity. The years rolled away, and he felt himself a small boy, with his father's hand on his head. Suddenly, in the distance, he saw a shining goldpiece against the darkness.

XX
THE MOON
IN PROXIMITY

HANS HARDT, reappearing in the control room, measured the angle at which the moon was shining, and from the result calculated the distance. "Another three thousand miles," he said. "We shall soon be starting our revolving course." He then ordered Anderl to remain on duty at the flywheels in order to keep the exhaust pipes directed toward the center of the moon.

The powerful wheels began to whir, the ship turned slowly over, and the moon appeared to sink until finally its great expanse was directly under the *Wieland*. On its side, now, the ship stormed through the ether.

Hardt kept in sight the chart showing the directions of the compasses. "In a minute our course will point five degrees east, passing the edge of the moon," he said to Anderl. "Look, our direction relative to the moon is changing more and more." Indeed the moon seemed to be turning about with tremendous speed. Each lofty mountain-top was easily discernible with the naked eye. The yellowish landscape extended under the *Wieland* beyond the field of vision.

Inasmuch as the vertical axis of the ship was pointed directly at the moon, their course was inclined obliquely toward it. The masses of this, the earth's satellite, seemed not only to rise out of the depths, but simultaneously to move sideways. The consequent impression was that the gigantic moon was rolling toward the *Wieland*.

As the ship approached nearer, this revolving motion affected the observers more strongly. They had to look away to avoid becoming dizzy from the extreme rapidity of this whirling mass.

"If we are fortunate," remarked Hardt steadily watching the instruments, "we shall be able to cut across the course of the satellite in such a manner that we shall meet it behind the moon in its next revolution. And yet," he mused, looking at the plot of their course, "the path which we have figured out does not exactly correspond."

Their present course ran close to the moon.

They were already skimming over the surface. Hardt shrugged his shoulders. "If the exhaust fails, we shall crash," he said gloomily, grasping the starting lever. The pumps began to hum and the liquid combustion substance was compressed into the vaporizer. Almost simultaneously a compression lever started the ignition, and the ship gave a sudden jerk. With a great clatter, tables and chairs fell to the floor, glasses smashed; and whoever was hovering without support at the moment was dashed to the floor in no gentle manner. Their goal was near.

"What in the world is going on?" cried Dr. Hardt, who had been smoking his pipe below, as he appeared in the control room much alarmed.

Hans Hardt vouchsafed no reply. He was busily studying the chart of their course. "It corresponds exactly," he said with a sigh of relief. "We shall glide past the moon at a distance of sixty-two and a half miles. We do not have to penetrate any air strata, and there is nothing to worry about for the time being." He then instructed Anderl to inspect the ship to see that no serious damage had occurred.

"That was the first shock," he said in satisfaction, as he pushed the fuel lever back to zero. "Were you greatly frightened, Uncle Alex?"

"Not so much. What happened to make everything fall to the floor so suddenly?"

"I had no time to give a warning. I hope no one was seriously injured."

"A few utensils are probably broken, and some of us may have bruises. But how is it that gravity returned and tore us out of the clouds at one stroke without any intermediate stage?"

Hardt laughed. "That word 'clouds' is well put. You are perhaps referring to the clouds of smoke with which you are prone to envelop yourself. As for the rest, it is all over now. This little impulse of gravity was only a small fraction of our normal terrestrial gravity. We have become spoiled by our sojourn in space and have forgotten how to use our natural means of locomotion."

"Will you not...?"

"Oh, look down there," said Hardt quickly.

"See how near to the old moon we are! It is no wonder we feel its influence."

"But why so suddenly and emphatically?"

"I let the secondary exhaust pipes work at half speed for ten seconds in order to veer our course a trifle. We made a small error in our calculations—that's all."

."And now?'

"We are coming much closer to the moon. Have your camera ready. You will take home such pictures as no roamer of the earth has ever displayed."

In the meantime, the moon was moving rapidly closer. It was exciting to watch the approaching mountains grow larger and clearer. New sections of level land appeared and shot past. One range of mountains seemed to overlap another, and the peaks to topple over one another. Only one who was not susceptible to dizziness could endure to watch the seemingly perpetual movement of the masses.

Dr. Hardt lay, as was his custom when watching the "world below," on his stomach at the window. "Hans," he cried in excitement, "how far are we from those graters down there?"

Hardt smiled at this ridiculous though not inept comparison. "Less than eighty miles, Uncle Alex. We shall approach to about sixty miles and then go upward again. If there were a layer of air about the moon, we would feel something of the heat of our speed."

The rotation of the "grater" slowed down and shifted into a sideward movement. Mountain ranges emerged over the distant horizon, approached and disappeared over the opposite edge of the moon. What a panorama! The sunlight grew dimmer. The deep crater valleys were in darkness, and only the mountain summits gleamed out of the twilight.

"It is evening in the region just below us," said Hardt.

The *Wieland* approached the division between the moon-day, equivalent to two earth-days, and the equally long moon-night.

Anderl finally appeared from his inspection trip, in apparent perturbation.

"What did you find below," inquired Hardt; "something broken down?"

"No, not that." "Everything is in order?"

"The few broken glasses and plates don't amount to much.

"Then why do you look as if you had lost your last friend?"

"Well, Tommy..."

"Have you two been quarreling again?" interrupted Hardt indignantly. "Haven't I told you you are not to do that any more? The American is here now and..."

"But, Mr. Hardt!" exclaimed Anderl. "He is not here at all!"

Hardt leaped to his feet. "What do you mean, Anderl? Where else could he be?"

The lad shrugged his shoulders and looked helplessly around. "I have scoured the ship. Tommy is gone for sure. I just found this slip of paper!"

Hardt, trembling with suspense, read the brief note: "I will alone bear the consequences of my action. T. B." That was all.

"The poor devil!" exclaimed Dr. Hardt.

"Now why did he do that? 1 should have thought him more considerate than that. Now he is dead, and the dead are always at fault."

"I didn't want that," murmured Hans Hardt.

"There might have been a balance of weight before landing."

"It is not yet certain that Tommy is dead," hinted Anderl, who was obviously reproaching himself. "He took along his pneumatic outfit, and that will keep him for a while."

"Let's do something about it," said Dr. Hardt in agitation. "Perhaps he is still hovering near by, and we can still save him."

• Otto Willi Gail

Hans Hardt gloomily shook his head.

"If the exhaust pipes had not been working in the interim, there would be some hope. We have changed our direction as well as our speed, however, and it is impossible now to estimate just where Tommy Bighead might be located."

Numerous telescopes were brought into play.

But there was no flicker of light on the firmament to indicate the whereabouts of Tommy. He had disappeared.

"It is terrible!" exclaimed Dr. Hardt softly.

"Just think of a man hovering, in total solitude, in the vastness of the Universe, with death staring him in the face and no hope of rescue. He will certainly go insane!"

"I could almost hope that he has already fallen to the moon and so found a speedy relief from such unthinkable torture," replied Hans Hardt. He added, "We might have treated him with more consideration. We owed so much to him. 1 tried to punish him for being a stowaway, and now 1 feel responsible! Poor Tommy!"

For a long time the engineer deliberated as to whether he ought to keep the exhaust pipes working and explore the endless space in an effort to find the unfortunate Tommy. There was not the slightest prospect of finding him, however, and the search would exhaust their fuel so that even the *Wieland* with its crew would be lost as well. It would not be worth while to sacrifice himself and his companions to find the reporter and be unable to help him even if they found him. He could not contemplate such a risk. And so, their helpless distress over the hideous fate of the American greatly curtailed their interest in the really remarkable trip around the moon.

"We shall soon see the lunar regions below us," said Hardt presently, "regions which no human eye has ever beheld." He was endeavoring to eradicate the apathetic depression which held the space travelers. "These gray mountains cover three-sevenths of the moon's surface. They have heretofore been entirely unknown, since the satellite never turns them toward the earth."

After examining the mountainous landscape, he turned to the compasses, adjusted the optic measuring scale, and observed the stretches of land passing before him. Unmistakable anxiety was evident on his countenance.

"What is happening now?" inquired Dr. Hardt.

"Remarkable! We have passed the point of our nearest approach to the moon, and now we should ascend."

"But..."

"There is no change in our distance from the moon's surface. It is becoming less rather than greater. Let us just wait patiently."

Slowly, yet perceptibly, they began a new approach. Beneath them the glittering mountain crests emerged from the twilight into the sunlight and flew past more rapidly. It was a sign that they were in nearer proximity. The engineer turned, with some agitation, to the measuring instruments. His glance moved back and forth between the optic scales and the moon's masses.

In fact, the view from the *Wieland*'s windows had become alarming. Dark, gigantic mountain ranges towered up from the horizon, toward which the spaceship was moving at a tremendous speed. The increasing darkness below intensified the gruesome spectacle. Ever alert, Hardt clutched the starting lever. Anderl kept the exhaust pipes perpendicular to the moon's surface. The mountainous masses loomed nearer and nearer, until Dr. Hardt cried out as the ship swooped over their summits, almost within reach of their grasp.

Immediately afterward, the landscape disappeared. The ship was directed once more away from the moon and the danger of a ricochet was safely past.

"Confound it! Something could have gone wrong there," said the Doctor, in evident relief as he looked back at the disappearing mountains.

"It seemed more dangerous than it really was," replied Hans Hardt. "The exhaust pipes would have snatched us away in time. It is better, though, that we came out all right without using them."

"What causes this deviation from our course?" asked Anderl thoughtfully.

"I don't think the course has changed. This second approach to the moon had a cause outside of the ship."

"The moon itself?"

"Probably. I have often wondered why the moon no longer rotates and faces the earth always on the same side. There are many explanations of that fact, but none seems really satisfactory. It seems to me that the opinion of the Viennese engineer, Hoerbiger, is the most authoritative. The moon is not like a ball, but is shaped somewhat like a hen's egg. This eggshaped body must necessarily have its heavy end, which would logically be the end turned toward the center of attraction, namely, the earth. For that reason, the moon appears like a circle to observers on earth, and no astronomer has yet been able to observe both ends.

"If you now consider that the *Wieland* streaked by the bright, larger portion of this 'egg' and then along the shaded section, and finally brushed the protruding rear portion on which cluster high mountains, the incidents of the last few minutes are plausibly explained."

"You may be right, Hans," replied Dr. Hardt, "but I hope that on our return trip we shall pass along the side of the moon at an appropriate distance, so that we shall be able to recognize its contours."

XXI
THE MYSTERIOUS SATELLITE

THE *Wieland* was enveloped in darkness. The sun had disappeared behind the moon, and the earth, which ordinarily would have distributed reflected light as the moon does to the earth, was obscured by the dark masses of the near-by cosmic body. The rocket plunged with stupendous speed into the shadow of the moon, whose surface receded into the darkness.

The space travelers had agreed on attempting to unravel the mystery of the small star, provided they could overtake it with an alloted amount of fuel. Now that Tommy Bighead was no longer a member of the party, the return to earth was assured with the amount of fuel which had originally been intended for it. The reserve supply could be utilized for exploration purposes.

The unaccustomed darkness, together mental and physical strain experienced during the last few hours, gave the travelers a feeling of overpowering drowsiness. With the operation of the exhaust for swinging the ship about in a circular course, hard on the trail of the satellite, the pressure became noticeably uncomfortable. Even if it did amount to only one-tenth the earth's gravity, the occupants of the ship were so unaccustomed to it that it oppressed them. Their limbs seemed weighted down. A pressure on the head seemed to paralyze their thoughts; and they were overcome with weariness.

Dr. Hardt soon lay in heavy slumber, which almost amounted to a stupor. Hans Hardt and Anderl fought against their fatigue. They must avoid flying blindly over the curved course, for that would make considerably more difficult their return to earth. The rocket was turned so that the exhaust pipes were directed toward their goal. The discharges were diminishing. It was, of course, a matter of bending back the parabolic curve through gradual decrease of speed. By keeping within the moon's orbit, its attraction could be put to advantage.

Anderl was almost in a doze when Hans Hardt's words aroused him. "The surface lies a little over four hundred miles below us. Our altitude is increasing slowly. I think that in a few minutes we can allow the *Wieland* to gravitate freely."

A soft, yellow light filtered into the control room. The earth emerged from behind the moon, spreading its enormous disc four times as large as that of the moon which illuminates terrestrial landscapes on clear nights.

Presently Hardt pushed the fuel lever completely back. The spaceship was hovering about five hundred miles above the moon mountains, and it was only gradually receding farther from them. Its course was firmly held by that of the moon, not in the form of a true circle, but a further decrease in speed made it impossible to overtake the satellite.

"With more precise adjustments we must wait until we come face to face with the satellite," commented Hardt. "Meanwhile there is nothing to do but allow the *Wieland* to gravitate in its present elliptical path, which will not deviate greatly from the desired circular path."

With the ship left once again entirely at the whim of nature, the pressure disappeared, and on awakening, Dr. Alexander Hardt found himself gently floating hither and thither about the room.

It was not long before the first burst of sunlight came through the windows. The cratercovered surface of the moon beneath them was aglow, and the spectacle of dawn on earth was reflected on the moon. The fiery crown of light enveloping the emerging earth disc, however, did not appear around the moon, which had no belt of atmosphere.

The two brilliant orbs floated below the ship, earth and moon in sharp competition. At present the moon, in its proximity and consequent fantastic size, overwhelmed the earth.

The crew was in high spirits. The pressure had disappeared, and with it their fatigue, which now seemed like a bad dream.

"Maybe the sun has gone mad," said Dr. Hardt, as he breakfasted with his nephew. "When he first honored us with his rays, he was down below. While we were hastening to Father Moon to tickle his beard a little, the sun was radiating splendor into the observation cabin; now he is squinting modestly at us from the side. I wouldn't have believed the central body of the solar system capable of such skipping about. The worst of it is that, with his eccentricities, he has had an effect upon old Mother Earth, whom I have always considered a trustworthy lady of ripe old age. To say nothing of the moon, this old bachelor goes his own way, and still has the audacity to make advances to Mother Earth."

"You seem to be in a very good humor, Uncle Alex," replied Hans Hardt, almost reproachfully. "It hasn't been long since you slipped into your hammock in a state of melancholy."

"Oh!" said the scientist with embarrassment.

"It was because I can't stand that awful gravity any longer."

"How do you expect to get along when we return home and Doctor Alexander Hardt will again weigh his one hundred and twenty pounds?"

"Keep still, Hans, I beg of you. It makes me fidgety to think about it. Couldn't we organize an expedition to Mars?"

The engineer laughed against his will. "Have you forgotten how you objected to being a member of this party? And now you want to explore the unknown realms of the planets!"

"That is explained by the inertia of matter, Hans. When I am seated, I am intent on remaining seated, and it is difficult for me to rise. But when I am wandering, I want to keep on wandering until some force holds me down. As a physicist and student of gravitation, you must understand that!"

Anderl, in the meantime, was sitting at the observation window, investigating the little dots of light on the satellite of the moon.

Through retardation and projection, determined by the direction they wanted to take, the travelers succeeded in keeping the *Wieland* at a distance of approximately fifteen thousand miles from the center of the moon, swinging in an elliptical course which was close to the orbit of the satellite. As the *Wieland* now had considerably greater speed than the satellite, it was inevitable that the latter must sooner or later be overtaken.

With some difficulty Anderl was keeping his gaze concentrated in the direction of their flight. He soon perceived against the side of the moon a glittering, rapidly approaching dot, which had been the object of their search. He immediately informed the commander of his discovery.

"We are in luck," cried the latter, his face flushing with pleasure. "The thing is gravitating parallel with us in our course." Adjusting the telescope, he added, "The difference in our speeds is apparently not great, and they can probably be equalized. It is too bad we do not know how large the body is, for the distance is too great to be measured with our optical scale."

Hardt waited half an hour in order to come a little nearer. He then gave his instructions. —

"Clear the way for maneuvers! Everybody in the hammocks!"

He had been seized by the exploration fever, and for the moment had forgotten about the ill-fated Tommy. He was the ship's commander, with a complicated but interesting task to perform, and the solution of the mystery occupied all his thoughts.

The rocket was directed toward the moon, and in this position the exhaust pipes functioned for ten seconds in order to bring it nearer the moon. The effect of gravity was immediately felt, and Dr. Hardt made the astonishing discovery that the great moon was no longer under the ship but high above the observation cabin.

"You are wrong, Uncle Alex," said Hans Hardt, without turning his attention from the scales and levers. Hit is not rising, but sinking."

"But the moon mountains are hanging way up there," he said as he pointed upward toward the window, which was letting in a brilliant light .

"That's a mere optical illusion, caused by the motors, which always signify 'below' when they are functioning."

The flywheels for altering position began to drone, and the *Wieland* again turned its torpedo-shaped hull parallel with the moon's surface, its exhaust pipes directed toward the speeding goal.

The moon's surface now appeared like a perpendicular wall, towering skyward from an endless depth. The ship appeared to be falling directly onto this wall. A yellow, gleaming surface projected upward wherever the eye wandered.

The flywheels hummed more frequently, slightly changing the direction as occasion required. At one moment a strong pressure would constrict the chest, at another the three men would rise, weightless, from their hammocks. The glimmering point of light hovering before them over the ball of the moon increased in size.

"That's a strange thing," said Hardt at the telescope. His voice was eager. "It appears like—like a collapsed dirigible, with a strong knot in the center. In any case, this little star has nothing in common with a rotating sphere. What do you think about it?" He let Dr. Hardt look through the telescope.

"That's right," agreed Dr. Hardt. "It looks like twin loaves, and they seem to be covered with ice. It is not rotating; it keeps the same side turned toward the moon. And it has remarkable contours. There, I see it more distinctly now. It seems to have a great, yawning fissure in the center, and on the side turned toward the moon a dark, circular spot as though a point were broken off. Right! Somewhat to the side, a smaller fragment is hovering."

"This satellite has apparently begun to disintegrate," said Hans Hardt in great excitement. "Maybe we are just in time to witness a falling star. Even though it is a small one, nevertheless, we are looking on at a spectacle which no other human being has ever seen."

"How can such a phenomenon dissolve so simply?" asked Anderl in the meantime.

"Who knows how many thousand years this fragment has been speeding about the moon? It is very small, and for that reason it resists the ether much better than larger masses. In imperceptibly smaller spirals, it has drawn nearer the center of attraction by a certain number of yards a decade. At present this satellite, the moon's moon, is hovering some sixty miles above the moon's surface. If the moon had an enveloping layer of air like the earth, the satellite would have long ago been checked in its speed by the air resistance, and fallen out of its course. The constant attraction of the moon has gradually deformed it, drawing it out lengthwise, and has checked its rotation on its axis. It is exactly like the earth's moon. It now appears to be near the point where its own density is not a sufficient counter-attraction. The centrifugal force of its rapid rotation is pulling it upward. The attraction of the moon in close proximity is drawing it downward. It is splitting. That is the fate of the moon. With the strong core in the middle it has kept moving. The fragments can continue to rotate in the original path near each other for a long time, split again, until they..."

He stopped short. "It is time for us to put on our pneumatic suits. Quick! I'll have to throttle soon and then the pressure will return."

They were at a distance from it of less than two miles. The three men, with their suits and helmets on, stood ready. The long-distance cables were attached to each other as an experiment, as any other means of communication between the men thus clothed was no longer possible.

"Is everything ready?"

The voices of his two companions replied. "That's all right, then," said Hardt. "As soon as we adapt our speed to that of the satellite, you slip out with me, Uncle Alex. There is no danger. We will gravitate freely, as we have no weight, and we will not fall off, in spite of the moon's nearness. And you, Anderl, continue to steer the rocket in order to prevent any fluctuations in speed until we have established a connection. This little star can't be more than thirty miles long. We shall have to throttle or we'll shoot past it. Get into the hammocks!"

The exhaust pipes pointed in the direction of their course. Three and four times the bluish stream of gas burst out. The mysterious satellite hovered quite near, though the intervening distance diminished slowly. Then it seemed to stand still, less than a hundred yards from the side of the *Wieland.*

The exhaust pipes had become silent. The courses were now exactly parallel. The spaceship and the satellite were gravitating around the moon in concentric, circular courses, and lay close to each other. They were like two express trains, racing at full speed.

"Now let's get over there quickly before the gap widens again," said Hardt, as he opened the door of the vault.

He and his uncle crept out. The cables were connected to the exterior of the ship. Then Anderl threw out a long coil of rope, fastened to the ship with steel bolts. Hardt fastened one end of the rope around his body.

"Are you ready, Uncle Alex?" he called. "Then drop down quickly, but be sure your direction is toward the satellite."

For a moment the Doctor struggled against a feeling of dizziness, and a great terror seized him before this tremendous abyss separating the *Wieland* from the cosmic creation. Here, with the broad expanse of the moon swimming like a glassy continent through space and seemingly almost within reach, all sense of security left him, and fear gripped him by the throat.

Suddenly Hans seized his reluctant uncle by the arm, bent his knees up like a sprinter about to start a race, and with a final glance in his direction jumped with all his might and main.

The two figures, inflated like toy balloons, glided rapidly out into the night. The suits shone brightly against the night sky. The telephone cable and the rope unwound like multicolored serpents. The rope ran smoothly off the coil. In the absence of gravity there was no resistance of any kind.

Anderl, left behind in the *Wieland,* followed with great interest the two figures which, breaking the force of their fall with pistol shots, arrived at the jagged satellite. They fastened the rope to a pointed protuberance, to which one of them clung, crept in, and drew his companion after him.

"The thing is hollow!" exclaimed Anderl to himself, and his mind puzzled over this fact.

The cable ran out to its full length. The explorers were apparently moving forward on the inside of this strange fragment of the Universe. Anderl was seized with uncontrollable curiosity. He slipped outside the ship and began to wind up the coil of rope in order to draw the *Wieland* nearer to the satellite.

The rocket and the satellite came together with a gentle crash.

XXII
PRIMEVAL RELICS

THE ice was brittle under Hardt's touch. When his eyes finally became accustomed to the semi-darkness inside the crevice, he beheld slabs of ice ripping apart, sundered walls, apparently a combination of ice with something else. Everything was crusted with ice. He pushed on. Partitions fell apart like decayed boards. He examined a fragment through the eyepieces of his helmet. It was wood—deep black, ebony wood. The veining could be distinguished.

His heart beat rapidly. Wood? Plant life here in universal desolation? How did it get here? Were there human beings-inhabitants of the moon? It was an unfathomable enigma. He was wholly absorbed in what he saw. He wanted to examine, to establish, then to form a conclusion.

He looked around for his companion, but the latter had crept farther into the interior of the—what?—of the moon's satellite? He followed after, slipping through an irregular hole. There were more jagged ice crevices. Then the light became brighter. With a single glance, he took in his surroundings. His heart almost stopped beating. Was he dreaming, or was this a hallucination of his overheated brain? A long, vaulted room; the walls decayed; yawning cracks letting in the sun; black walls—ebony wood! In yellow, glittering sections he perceived dovetailed metal slabs. He scraped off the ice, and lo, gold glittered under his gaze—pure, shining gold!

An altar, with a figure on a red marble pedestal—also gold. Ebony wood, red marble and gold. Priceless treasures—buried in

the silent cosmos.

Splinters of strange furniture floated from the ground, aroused from eternal slumber by the touch of man.

This was no heavenly body—No! It was a habitat of mankind! How did they get here? By spaceship?

Dr. Hardt, clinging to a projection, was closely examining a golden slab. On it was engraved a picture—a man's head, with long skull and oblique, almond eyes. A clumsy design! And on the forehead a mark. The Doctor bent closer. The mark was a sign-a cross-and on it a circle. "The holy hieroglyph of life!" he whispered. "The key to the Pharaohs' Nile dwellings; the life tree of the Maya tribes; the holy sign of the Brahmans; the primeval symbol of .all earthly races!"

And under the picture were inscriptions, in strange characters reminding one of Phœnician script. The Doctor fixed the outline of these symbols in his memory so that he might try later to decipher the meaning.

"Great heavens!" exclaimed Hans Hardt, overwhelmed. "Where are we? What does all this mean?"

"We have had a glimpse into the fabled dawn of history," replied Dr. Hardt seriously. "What we see is part of a culture which disappeared thousands of years ago, a culture of antediluvian tribes, the origin of all races on earth."

"But how did it all get here..."

They were interrupted by a sudden thud, which jarred the decayed walls of the enclosure so that they burst apart in the middle, letting in a flood of sunshine through the broad cleavage.

Hardt was filled with a grim foreboding. The rocket! What had happened to it? Even now Anderl's voice came through the telephone. "Mr. Hardt! Come back, quick!"

"What's the matter, Anderl?"

"The *Wieland* has struck. I am afraid there is a leakage..." His voice trembled in agitation and fright.

Hardt sprang into action. He dashed back to the opening through which he had entered. There loomed the spaceship hard against the splitting satellite. The rear end of the exhaust pipe was buried deeply in a jagged crack. A shapeless mass was climbing around it—Anderl.

"Good heavens, Anderl!" exclaimed Hardt, horrified. "What have you done!"

"I wound up the rope in order to get nearer. I didn't stop to think that the motion couldn't be stopped. I intended to move the ship around with the exhaust pipes toward the protuberance and then throttle it down. But it was too late. The *Wieland* got away from me. I hope..."

Hardt waited for no further explanation from the incoherent Anderl. He hastily went over to the wedged-in end of the ship and began to chip off the ice around it. A bluish streak of frozen gas shot out. In the collision, a sharp fragment of the satellite had penetrated the hull of the *Wieland* and burst open one of the tanks filled with liquid hydrogen. And now the precious stuff was evaporating into the Universe.

The engineer gazed despairingly at the broad gaping hole. With no fuel, there would be no return. Everything was lost! For a second he pondered. It was impossible to repair the leak, as the interior of the tank was not accessible. On the outside, the great force of the issuing gas prevented any speed in repair. It would take hours to patch the opening, and in the meantime the total contents of the tank would have leaked out.

What could he do? The earth was an immeasurable distance away, so that a rapid return was out of the question. The moon—that was near. It would not require much motor power to counteract its comparatively slight gravitational attraction. They could perhaps reach it before it was too late. The remaining supply of gas was certainly sufficient to break their fall and enable a smooth landing. Even after reaching the moon, they would be on a barren body, destitute of atmosphere and of any kind of resource. He must not hesitate, however. There was no choice! They must work very quickly! Every moment counted!

"Back to the ship right away, Anderl! Uncle Alex! Quick! There is danger!" shouted Hardt into the telephone, as he hurried to the window of the *Wieland*.

In the interim Dr. Hardt had made a disturbing discovery in the interior of the satellite. Trembling with fright, he gazed into the jagged enclosure. What was that lying here? Shapeless, bloated limbs—a body—was it a human being? A ghost? A mummy from some primeval age, preserved in a coating of ice? He was so excited that his vision blurred. He was fearfully approaching the gruesome figure when Hardt's voice shouted through the telephone. He stood for a moment as if paralyzed.

"Alex, Alex, where are you? Come right back if you value your life. There's no time to lose!" The voice of the ordinarily calm engineer was that of a man pursued by bloodhounds.

Dr. Hardt hesitated for another second. Here was a precious discovery-one which would cause a furor in the whole scientific world. Should he leave it lying there? Instinctively, hardly aware of what he was doing, he lifted the ice-crusted body, and dragging it after him, emerged through the opening.

XXIII
THE DESCENT
TO THE MOON

THE *Wieland* swayed in a practically unaltered position near the fateful satellite. Only a slight swinging motion had been caused by the force of the escaping gas.

"Off with your helmets!" commanded Hardt.

"They will smother you."

Dr. Hardt obeyed without a question.

The flywheels whirred, and gradually the ship turned about until the exhaust pipe was at an angle with the direction of their movement. At the same moment the pilot pushed the fuel lever.

The rocket rapidly departed from the satellite.

As the distance increased, the cosmic creation dwindled into a minute flicker of light. After a minute, the gravitational speed of the *Wieland* diminished, until its circular course swerved toward the moon and it descended in a free fall. For a period of two more minutes Hardt left the exhaust pipes disconnected.

"Our speed will increase again," he said, "but this is the only possible means of effecting a landing in the short time which presumably is left to us."

He gave Anderl instructions to keep the exhaust pipe directed constantly toward the moon. "Do not neglect this, Anderl, whatever happens."

Dr. Hardt was on duty at the optical distance scale.

Their distance from the surface of the moon now amounted to two hundred and fifty miles, and their falling speed was about a mile and a half a second. With burning eyes, Hardt watched the masses of the moon, approaching with ominous speed.

"Watch out! Now we are beginning to throttle!" he shouted, and pushed the fuel lever far ahead. A strong vibration jarred the ship. The speedometer needle advanced, and pressure bore down upon the three men like an invisible curtain. They were going slower now. Was the distance sufficient to bring them to a complete stop? The exhaust pipes were functioning properly, but could they check the terrific speed downward with the remaining fuel power? If they could not sufficiently throttle the speed, the *Wieland* would crash on the moon mountains.

If they used too much power, their fuel would be exhausted before the rocket could reach the safety of the moon's surface, and again, a fatal drop would result. Danger threatened them in either case.

Hardt's brain worked like lightning. Their speed was being reduced at the rate of about eighty feet a second. By the end of forty seconds' operation of the exhaust pipes, the rate of retardation was over three thousand feet per second. He looked down again. A shimmering, yellowish surface, extended below the ship, cut by dark lines. On one side, a great circular mountain range enclosed a huge crater valley.

. "We are landing on a familiar section," thought Hardt.

An irregular array of jagged mountain tops appeared to hasten over the horizon line. The field of vision became more restricted. It seemed as if the land were fleeing from one spot to the various points of the compass; and this spot was the one toward which their ship was falling.

Their altitude was called out at regular intervals. "Six and a quarter miles! Four and a half miles!" and so on. Slowly they approached land, and yet they were falling too fast. In twenty seconds more their fate would be decided.

Hardt compressed his lips. Did he dare to do it? He would wait five more seconds. "Three thousand, two hundred and fifty feet!" announced Dr. Hardt in a croaking voice. "Two thousand, two hundred and seventy-five! One thousand, three hundred!..."

"Now!" cried Hardt, as he shoved the fuel lever to its limit. Full fuel was going to the exhaust pipes. Five enormous streams of fire belched downward, opposing tremendous resistance to the surface beneath. The landscape seemed to yield. The speedometer indicator tore across the red mark. The hammocks creaked. The space travelers lay like crushed worms on the floor of the control room. Their breasts showed no evidence of breathing. Every heart seemed to have stopped beating for the moment.

Anderl clung to the switchboard, holding himself up with superhuman effort. Lights danced before his eyes; a fiery millstone weighed on his chest; his ribs felt as if they were being pulverized. There, between rifting blue veils, appeared the fuel lever. He seized it between his teeth, pushed it back, and then sank heavily down.

The terrific pressure, of three seconds' duration, had broken chairs and flattened out cans of preserves. Moreover, it had destroyed a single life-their small feathered companion, the yellow canary, lay dead in its cage, its little heart stopped forever.

Hardt wearily picked himself up. "Thanks, Anderl," he said. "Five more seconds, and none of us would have..." He looked out of the window. "We are all right!" he called, giving a sigh of relief, as he passed his hand over his feverish brow.

The *Wieland* had come to a stop barely sixty-five feet above the ground. Under the remaining slight pressure from the exhaust pipes, it was beginning to rise. The rest of the landing was easy.

Cautiously, a millimeter at a time, Hardt shoved back the fuel lever. With spitting exhausts, the rocket hovered for a moment at a tower's height from the ground. Finally, like a fluttering leaf, it sank down and with a gentle thud struck the surface of the moon. Simultaneously the exhaust went dead.

"We are safe for the time being!" exclaimed Hardt. "However, we are in a desolate country where no man's foot has yet trod. And we cannot go back."

XXIV
THE SECRET
OF THE MUMMY

THE mood of the travelers, in spite of their successful landing, was not merry. A host of doubts and uncertainties as to their exact situation prevented them from reaching any clear decision, for the moment at least.

For some minutes the three men crouched silently in their ship's narrow observation cabin. Half deaf from the recent pressure, each was sunk in his own troubled thoughts. Anderl's conscience weighed heavily upon him for having caused such a catastrophe through his carelessness. Tommy Bighead's method of joining the party seemed a harmless joke in comparison with the guilt which he had brought upon himself by his stupidity. He would have been willing to cut off his right hand, could this have done any good to their situation.

Dr. Hardt's thoughts were still with the mysterious satellite circling about the moon. Where did this thing come from? How did it get there?

How old could it be? His mind was so occupied with questions of archeological interest that he scarcely took note of his present surroundings.

Hans Hardt's thoughts concerned the future.

They had made their safe landing on the moon, sound in mind and body. Their fuel, however, was almost entirely exhausted. How were they to get away?

"The main thing now is to eat," declared Anderl. "We can't stand this with an empty stomach!"

Anderl was right, and he forthwith began to investigate the

cans of food.

Deep in thought, Hardt looked out the window onto this strange world where they had been cast by fate. A level, yellowish white surface stretched before him. It was covered with irregular lines and darker surfaces which looked like lakes. Farther away, sharp, solitary, conical mountain peaks rose abruptly from the plain, as though scattered about by some divinity in a playful mood. In the background, towering above black shadows, was a lofty, cleft mountain wall, apparently a uniform range, which cut off the view from everything beyond. Even this mountainous wall was studded with numerous abruptly rising, conical peaks, which looked as though they were covered with flour. These fantastic prongs glittered with dazzling brilliance against the dark, cloudless sky. A weird, steely green, though bright light, layover the strange landscape. No breeze stirred; and deathly stillness reigned.

Judging from the oblique position of the cabins, the *Wieland* must have leaned sideways during its descent and landed in a slant, resting on its rear end.

"So this is the moon," said Hardt slowly.

"And we are the first human beings to view its wonders."

"Hans! Hans!" called Dr. Hardt in a voice betraying great excitement. "Look here!"

Turning around, Hans beheld the scientist kneeling before the shapeless, ice-crusted body which he had brought with him from the mysterious satellite. During the strain of the descent his discovery had been left unheeded, and it was only now that Dr. Hardt had thought to examine the mummy.

"Take a look at this thing!" said Dr. Hardt in agitation as he chipped the ice away. "That looks like—like a—a diver's helmet!"

Hardt leaned down with sudden interest.

"Indeed!" he exclaimed, now showing astonishment. "The body is encased in an armor which looks exactly like our pneumatic outfits!" On reflecting a moment, he added, "It may be that some luckless spaceship came to grief on that satellite, though it seems inconceivable. Anderl, bring a pair of pliers!"

The frosted screws finally yielded, and the heavy helmet was removed. "Good heavens, a real man!" exclaimed the men in unison. A blue, bloated face, with broad forehead and strong cheekbones, met their gaze.

"Get off that suit before it is too late!" cried Dr. Hardt. He laid his ear to the breast of the unknown. "He is still alive! God be thanked! He is still alive!"

Resuscitation methods were at once begun under the directions of the Doctor. The rigid organism began to revive with the systematic movement of the arms. His breast began to heave, and presently his eyes opened, his lips moved.

Dr. Hardt bent over and held his ear close to the moving lips. Tears of joy streamed down his cheeks as he made out the words, "What's up?" Tommy—it was actually Tommy Bighead who had been rescued!

"Here was I, hoping to unwrap a mummy of the primeval age," said Dr. Hardt in apparent indignation, to hide his emotion, "and Tommy turned up, which is better yet. Tommy, is it really you? Are you all right?"

"Of course I am!" answered Tommy weakly. "There's an awful pain in the back of my head, and—in my left thumb."

It looked as if the friction of the suit had caused him some discomfort, for a wide, red welt spread over his left hand like a burn. In reality, the painful, though insignificant, wound was caused by the extreme cold.

In a short time Tommy had recovered to the extent of being able to stand up. He looked questioningly from one to another, and then his broad face lighted up with a smile. "I certainly am glad to see you again," he exclaimed. "Is this Heaven or Hell?"

"This isn't Heaven by any means," replied Anderl, "but something on that order. We're on the moon. Just look at it! And now you'll get a pig's rib to eat," he added, smacking his lips in anticipation of the forthcoming treat. "You were puffed up and stylish all right, but I guess you won't sneak out again without thinking it over. "You big cuckoo!" he muttered in affectionate rebuke as he disappeared into the kitchen to prepare the best breakfast that the depleted supplies of the *Wieland* could afford.

"Not too much," shouted Hardt after him.

"There's no telling how long we shall have to live on what we have."

As Dr. Hardt gently bound up Tommy's wounds, Hans stood gazing earnestly at the face of the rescued reporter.

"That was the strangest adventure ever experienced by man, or ever to be experienced, Mr. Bighead!" The latter nodded.

"It will have a front page in the *Michigan Evening Post*, with glaring headlines: 'The Living Meteor, or, Tommy Bighead's Journey into the Fourth Dimension,' and so on. The competition will be a riot! And Mr. Tiller will be bursting with pride in the best reporter in the State of Michigan! Did I say Michigan? No! In the whole world! And I don't mean maybe!"

Hardt smiled. "You certainly deserve the title of best reporter in the world, Mr. Bighead! But tell us about it. How did you land on the satellite?"

"Oh, that was simple. I just wanted to relieve you of my presence and be the only one to suffer for what I had done. So I took along some oxygen and cartridges, and started off in some direction, I don't know just which. The trip was mighty cold and uninteresting. I went to sleep for a while. When I awoke, an enormous, shining object was coming toward me from the side. Of course I shot at it—used almost all my cartridges. It was like an elephant hunt. I landed with a thump and grabbed onto a crevice. My arm is still lame from the jerk. I crept inside the crevice and settled down for a nap. You know the rest better than I."

"It's a real miracle," commented Hardt. "It is not so strange that your flight path crossed the path of the satellite; but your arriving at the intersection point at exactly the moment the satellite was passing is a lucky coincidence on which I would not have staked a penny against a million. How many times did you fire your pistol before landing?"

"I don't exactly know. There may have been over a hundred rounds."

"Well! Every shot alters a man's speed by one hundred and fifty centimeters a second. One hundred shots would hasten or

retard your motion by about four hundred and ninety feet a second."
After calculating for a few moments, he continued, "That's right.
The difference between your speed and the satellite's could have
been no greater than approximately five hundred and fifty feet a
second. It is not, therefore, an occult phenomenon. Your rescue
can be explained by natural laws, and even proved mathematically.
But it is still a miracle!"

"Or an evidence of Divine Providence!" softly interpolated
Dr. Hardt.

"Phenomenon, miracle, Providence? Very nice-sounding
words," replied Tommy drily. "They'd sure make a hit in my article,
'Tommy's Journey into Nothingness.' Like fun! When do we start?"

"Where?"

"Home, of course!"

"Either within ten days, or— "

"Or...?"

"Or not at all," gravely answered Hardt.

"How so? Do you intend to establish a colony here on the
moon? I'll take over the editorship of the Moon Courier."

"Our present situation is no joke, Mr. Bighead!"

"Well, I find it a heap more comfortable than on that wreck of
a satellite up there."

A fragrance of coffee aroma came from the kitchen.

"As long as the sun shines," said the engineer, "we can survive
here. Until the sun reaches the zenith, our location is in the east.
Fortunately a day on the moon is the equivalent of two weeks on
earth. If a lunar night catches us here, we shall be cut off from
heat for two weeks, and death from freezing would be inevitable."

"Then let's start before then."

"We are all of the same inclination, Mr. Bighead. But our fuel
tanks are empty, and unless we can create some sort of fuel here,
there will be no returning for us, and these wilds will be both our
new home and our grave."

XXV
AN UNKNOWN LAND

DURING breakfast the four men deliberated over ways and means. "Before we abandon the ship," said Hardt, "we must ascertain exactly where we are."

"On the moon," interrupted Tommy. "Is there any doubt about that?"

"That is understood. The moon, however, is not a mathematical point, but a planet with a circumference of more than six thousand miles, big enough to hold all America."

"Humph! I'd like to know how you're going to find out on what part of the planet we are."

"That is not difficult, if we can see the earth.

In the event that our home planet is visible from here, then by all the laws of nature we are located on the side of the moon turned toward the earth, which is naturally the most familiar region."

At these words, three pairs of eyes promptly turned toward the windows.

"If that flat crescent up there is not the earth," said Tommy pointing upward, "I'll eat tripe for the rest of my life and never write another line."

In fact, against the black depths of the sky appeared the vague outline of a huge, dully-gleaming portion of a disc. The sun seemed tiny in comparison with its great magnitude. The familiar contours of Europe and part of Asia were distinguishable with the naked eye.

Hardt adjusted the sextant and then began to calculate

according to his observation of the earth's disc. Half of the distance from the upper to the lower edge gave the distance between the moon's horizon and the middle of the earth.

"If we consider the moon's outer edge, as seen from the earth on the night of a full moon, its equator, the distance to the earth gives our position relative to this equator in degrees, which is, therefore, our approximate latitude. I find it to be 80 degrees and 40 minutes. In that case, we are very near the center of the known lunar disc. The distance to the earth indicated that this center was 90 degrees, and we are about six and a half degrees from it."

Hardt unfolded a large astronomical chart.

Around the center point he drew a circle with a radius of about six and a half degrees. "Somewhere on this circle," he explained to his interested companions, His our present location. As you see, the circle runs close to the large, circular range called Rhæticus, cuts through the Hipparcus mountains, touches the Herschel and MacLaurin crater, and continues for some distance through a plain, finally descending here through the middle of the Triesnecker crater."

"That's very interesting," said Dr. Hardt. "Our exact location is still rather indefinite, however."

"Have patience! There is still another means of determining our location; that is, by reckoning the distance of the Polar Star. Fortunately, on the black background, the brighter stars can be seen in the daytime. Just look for the seven-star constellation of the Little Bear. You all know that, certainly."

"No, I don't," frankly admitted Tommy. "The last star in the tail of the Little Bear is the Polar Star, which always lies directly above the earth's North Pole. It can also be considered as an indicator of direction from the moon. Any small variation can easily be made right by arithmetical calculation."

It was some time before Anderl had any success in his study of the stars gleaming over the mountain-bound horizon.

Hardt mused to himself. "Only four degrees and thirty minutes."

"And how is that measurement going to help us?"

"In this way. The latitude of the moon's north pole is ninety degrees; of the belt-line lying midway between the north and south poles it would be zero. By measuring our distance from the north pole, we have the distance of our present location from the belt-line. On this map, the belt-line appears as a horizontal dividing line through the middle of the moon's disc. If we now draw a parallel line through the northern hemisphere at a distance of four and a half degrees from the belt-line, our location must lie in the former line."

"And that straight line cuts our circle at two points," added Dr. Hardt, Hand on one of those two points we are standing at the present moment. Isn't that right?"

"Quite right. Now let us examine the two points in question. The eastern point lies in a broad plain. Through our windows we see mountains, not very far distant. That eliminates the eastern point. Now the western point—look, it lies in the middle of the Triesnecker crater!"

"What?" exclaimed Tommy in astonishment.

"Don't tell me we are in a crater! That's impossible. This is a plain, not a crater cavity."

"Why not? Of course, the so-called moon craters are not like our volcanic craters on earth. In most cases they are level areas, rather than deep cavities; and often they extend into long valleys, enclosed by great, circular mountain ranges. Look around. The entire horizon is bounded by an unbroken chain of mountains. There is no doubt that we are in the Triesnecker crater, and that is an agreeable discovery."

"I don't see what there is so agreeable about that!" muttered Tommy, still unconvinced. "Can you see how we are going to get out of this crater?"

"From two standpoints this region is favorable for our present situation, Mr. Bighead. In the first place, the crater is quite well known. We can find photographs of this whole region in our atlas of the moon. We can't lose our way on this expedition, that's one thing certain. Secondly—look!"

As Tommy shook his head in bewilderment, Hardt joyfully pointed to one of the many scales on the switchboard. "Read downward!"

"Eighty millimeters. Well, what of it?"

"Don't you suspect anything yet?"

"No!"

"Well, this scale gives the reading of the outside barometer. There is an air pressure of eighty millimeters!"

"Even so!" said Tommy, still unenlightened. "Don't you grasp how important that fact is for us? It means that there is air outside. To be sure, there is not much, and it is eight times as thin as that of the earth. But there is air, nevertheless, oxygen!"

"Then we can go out without our pneumatic suits?" asked Anderl in uncertainty.

"No, Anderl, not that. The pressure is much too weak. Our veins would burst with one-third less pressure than we are accustomed to on earth. In any event, there is the possibility of pumping into our ship any amount of air that we need, and we can preserve our supplies in liquid air for the return trip. That means something! Furthermore, where there is air, there must be water; and perhaps there is some sort of life—who knows?"

"Isn't that a contradiction of all we learned in school about conditions on the moon? Isn't the lack of air a completely established fact?"

"Certainly, Uncle Alex! It is a long time since the moon has had a real air mantle. If there were one, we should have felt it on landing. But that does not exclude the fact that there are still some remains of air in deep crater valleys. This is probably the case in our Triesnecker crater. You see for yourself. I think we may be prepared for all sorts of surprising discoveries."

The next important thing was to explore the near vicinity of the spaceship. This first sally into unknown conditions could hide unforeseen dangers, and no one of the four men wished to remain behind.

"There is no use in all four of us going out at once," Hardt insisted. "Four men do not see any more than two. Moreover, we need a dependable guard in the ship. One can never tell what is going to happen in this old moon."

It was finally decided that Dr. Hardt and the injured Tommy

should remain in the *Wieland*.

"We shall not stay out longer than two hours," said Hardt, as he slipped into his suit and attached the various instruments. "You can pass the time by taking photographs. Don't leave the ship under any condition."

"O.K.," said Tommy, still munching his pork chop. "I'll take a little nap in the meantime."

Hardt and Anderl crept out through the vault and climbed to the ground by means of a rope ladder.

XXVI
ICE, AND MORE ICE

THE *Wieland* lay near the almost perpendicular wall of a small, cone-shaped mountain which, with several other such "cones," formed an independent group.

"When we come back," said Hardt to Anderl through the speaking tube, "we must thoroughly inspect the ship and, more important, mend the leak. Still more essential, however, is something else that we have to do."

He struck a match. It flickered feebly and went out. The proof, nevertheless, was sufficient to indicate the presence of oxygen in the ether; otherwise, the match would not have flamed at all.

The two men were standing on a dark, crystalline substance which was ice. The entire valley basin was apparently encrusted with ice. Numerous narrow, deep fissures extended over the surface like glacier cleavages. Bright, whitish spots denoted powdered ice, which covered, also, the distant peaks and ridges, giving them the appearance of being snow-capped. Brilliant sunshine contrasted with deep shadow; and above all this stretched a canopy of darkness studded with gleaming stars .

Hardt stood silent for a time, lost In contemplation of the amazing landscape. It was like a setting for a fairy tale.

Anderl, who frequently on earth had roamed through regions of perpetual ice and snow, and had climbed to the wonder of snow-capped mountains, felt more or less at home.

"It's like being on a glacier!" he exclaimed.

"The higher one climbs, the darker becomes the sky and the brighter the snow-covered peaks. I have seen nothing as impressive as this, though!"

"The sky naturally appears darker as the strata of air over the observer become thinner. That is no novelty to fliers and space travelers. But that's not all. Take a good jump upward, Anderl!"

Anderl obediently jumped, with sufficient force to carry him about six feet high on earth. It was different here. He could easily have reached the roof of a four-story building. It took him five full seconds to land again on the Ice.

"That's fine, Anderl! If you made such a leap before your comrades in Friedrichshafen, you surely would have the title of world's champion jumper."

"It probably won't be so easy when I weigh one hundred and seventy pounds again. How much does that amount to here on the moon?"

"Just a sixth of your normal weight on earth.

Ordinary strength makes us as powerful as Titans in this locality."

With gigantic steps, each exceeding thirty feet, the men moved rapidly over the ice plain. They stepped across a twenty-foot crevice as casually as a city-dweller steps over a gutter.

"The ice cover must be very thick," said Hardt in a disappointed tone. "We cannot judge where the rock strata begin. They would interest me more than ice does."

Suddenly Hardt halted and pointed to a small dark spot. "Water, Anderl! It is really open water. It doesn't seem possible!"

Anderl didn't see why anything so ordinary as water should cause excitement, and was about to proceed on his way. But Hardt held him fast.

"Go very slowly. And no violent motion!" he commanded, as he crept cautiously to the edge of the pool. Drawing a magnifying glass from his pocket, he held it in the sun above the mirrorlike surface of the water. Presently the water began to bubble where the light was reflected, before long the whole pool was boiling. Thick clouds of steam enveloped the men. Anderl drew back involuntarily.

"You don't need to move," said Hardt with a laugh.

"But the water is boiling."

"Of course it is boiling!" Hardt held a small thermometer in the dense steam. "Seven degrees Centigrade [44.6 Fahrenheit].. We won't get scalded in that!"

The vapor became thinner and fell to the ground in a large ring. The pool had vanished, frozen!

"That's funny!" marveled Anderl. "The water boils while it is cold?"

"Boils and freezes at the same time," said Hardt. "That seems astonishing to us, but it is easily explainable. With the low pressure of this thin atmosphere, water does not boil at one hundred degrees Centigrade, but at seven or eight degrees. The freezing and boiling points, therefore, are not far apart, and water can exist only in the range of temperature between zero and eight degrees. As a consequence, liquid water is very unstable. Below zero it forms ice; above eight degrees it forms steam, which immediately freezes into fine icicles. There is no cause for surprise, therefore, if water is a rarity on this barren planet. Only where there is a trace of air, and a resulting pressure, can there be water, and then only if the sun happens to produce a temperature between zero and eight degrees.

"There is no possibility of seas, for there is scarcely any vapor. The process of evaporation withdraws such quantities of heat from the regions in which water boils, that freezing begins very near the boiling point, and evaporation is almost immediately checked. Yes, this is a strange land!"

"I am surprised," said Anderl, "that the sun does not melt these masses of ice. It shines continuously for two weeks without hindrance of clouds. I should think it would be as hot as Hades here."

"As the sun goes higher, the temperature in our crater valley will probably become warmer, but I doubt if it will be that warm," replied Hardt. "The moon has a very thin mantle of air, and for that reason the heat is not prevented from radiating into the Universe. Even on earth the summer temperature would drop at least seventy degrees if there were no air mantle, and our planet,

too, would be a region of ice and snow. It is not alone the radiation of the sun which causes this. A planet must know how to retain the heat bestowed upon it.

"Our earth is particularly fortunate in its natural conditions. Dense atmosphere and comparative nearness to the sun result in a bountiful supply of heat; yet it is far enough from the sun not to suffer from the fine ice drifts which the sun, because of its radiation pressure, scatters in all directions throughout the Universe.

"Even on earth, we have our snow-covered mountains which are not affected by the summer sun, in the very tropics near the equator. This is generally attributed to the protecting layer of air which separates the snow from empty space. Where we are now, the air is much thinner than on top of the Himalayas, for example. However that may be, the scientists will be able to build up a conclusive theory from our observations."

Hardt and Anderl wandered for an hour, and everywhere they found-Ice! Blocks, projecting points, crevasses, towering masses, huge icicles reminding one of stalactitic formations, occasional channels or pools of water which quickly froze. Time after time a mist of vapor would suddenly arise from nowhere and as suddenly sink to the ground in the form of hoar frost. Nowhere was there a spot of bare ground to be seen, nor was there any trace of plant or animal life. One could not judge from this restricted area, however, whether the entire surface of the moon lay under a crust of ice.

The enchantment of the fairy-like winter landscape did not hold the two explorers for long. A mere blade of grass or a fragment of stone would have held for Hardt much more significance than the imposing splendor of the ice formations.

"It seems we have to be satisfied with ice," remarked Hardt, shading his eyes from the glare of the sun. "We shall have to stake our hope on ice and water."

"When one stops to think," muttered Anderl, "that we are tramping around on the one thing we need most badly, without being able to use it, it is enough to send one wild."

"Yes, yes, Anderl! Here is ice, in inexhaustible quantities; and ice is frozen water; and water is a chemical combination of hydrogen and oxygen—just what we need. If we could only dissolve it, we should have enough fuel for our rocket, and getting out of this desolate world would be mere sport."

"We mustn't think about it."

"Indeed we must think about it, Anderl! Ice is our only hope. We must find ways and means of making oxyhydrogen gas out of ice. Think of nothing else, Anderl. Our whole life depends upon the solution of this problem!"

"It would be quite simple with electrolysis, and the ship's generator produces..." "Enough for our need if put into full action," was the quick reply. "But what shall we feed it, Anderl? That is the question."

Anderl thought with concentration.

"A crank movement to be operated by hand might be installed."

"Yes, but we might work every day for months before producing, with our limited strength, a sufficient amount of fuel. We haven't that much time. Night will be here in ten days at the latest. If we are caught here, we shall surely freeze to death. Aside from that, our supplies won't hold out more than 'fourteen days, even with the most frugal economy."

"Is there no source of energy in this strange land? Coal? Carbide?"

Hardt shrugged his shoulders. "It is possible. But where? And how can we find a sufficient amount in such a short time?"

"Well, of course! That wouldn't do, anyway," retorted Anderl.

"There is a source of energy here, Anderl, a great and inexhaustible source of energy!"

Anderl looked inquiringly through his helmet, but could not make out the face of the engineer. "I meant the sun," continued Hardt.

"That's right! The sun! It shines here continuously, and much more powerfully than on earth. That will do!"

"Don't go so fast! It is not so simple. We must go step by step. For concentration of the sun's rays we have that large concave mirror coated with silver leaf, that we used as a telescope on the way here. There are still some rolls of silver leaf left, with which

153

we can easily make more mirrors. If that is not enough, we can unscrew the objective glasses from all the telescopes and turn them into condensing lenses. With all these condensers we can concentrate the heat of the sun on one point."

"Good! And under the focus we shall have a vessel of water," supplemented Anderl enthusiastically. "We can use one of the empty oxygen containers for that, and it will withstand the pressure of the steam."

"Yes, that's so! So far, everything is clear. The next question is how to turn the steam thus produced into motor power. All we need is a steam turbine."

"Perhaps we might be able to reconstruct the gas motor for the electrical system," ventured Anderl, and he began to recall what resources the tool chest might offer.

"We'll try that, anyway, Anderl. Here is a problem which will show what you can do as a mechanic. In the long run, it is always better to undertake something that seems hopeless than nothing at all."

Anderl was already so deep in his problem that he was no longer listening to Hardt.

"If we can produce enough steam with the mirrors to drive the motor, we shall then have an electric current to decompose water. Then comes a new difficulty..."

"Stop, stop!" cried out Anderl, as he drew Hardt backward by the telephone cable.

While they were talking, the two men had arrived at the group of conical mountains and had crossed the first chain with little effort. Now they were at the edge of a jagged precipice, and Hardt had nearly fallen off. To his astonishment, he discovered that this particular group of mountains surrounded a funnel-like opening, somewhat on the order of a small crater within the large Triesnecker crater valley. The opening had a diameter of perhaps nine hundred and seventy-five feet. Walls of ice descended precipitously to an incalculable depth where no light penetrated. The bottom was invisible through the obscurity. From the point where the walls plunged into darkness issued a thin, white vapor.

"If this opening reaches down beyond the ice layer," said Hardt after careful consideration, "we should have a gateway through which to penetrate the solid body of the moon. That would interest my uncle. Do you think, Anderl, that anyone could go down there?"

"That's simple! With a sharp ice pole and a rope, we shall be prepared to climb down the wall. I have done much more difficult things. It will be a help not to weigh very much. But it's quite misty down there!"

"In three days the sun will be at its zenith, directly above us. Perhaps then its rays will reach far enough to illuminate the bottom of the precipice. Until then we must put an end to our explorations."

Hardt stepped curiously onto the curved edge of the mysterious funnel, but decided to return to the ship.

"We have much to do, Anderl, and we mustn't waste any time!"

XXVII
MOTIVE POWER

FOR the next few hours the little colony on the moon worked feverishly on the construction of a sun-power station. Much-needed sleep was out of the question.

The *Wieland*'s observation cabin was converted into a workshop. Hour after hour Anderl filed and hammered and perspired in the process of taking apart the motor and reconstructing it in such a way that it might be adaptable for operation by steam. Under his skillful hands, the parts fitted together precisely according to the engineer's plans. Hardt himself was surprised at the superior skill of Anderl, on whose work hung the life of four men.

Tommy Bighead, who had no special technical ability, made himself useful as general handy man, even to the point of presiding in the kitchen. Dr. Hardt worked with his nephew outside on the ice.

After a few minor repairs were made on the rocket, and the leak in the hydrogen tank mended, huge concave mirrors were set up beside the ship on the steep mountain wall against which it leaned. The mirrors converged the sun's rays onto one spot. Under this focus Hardt set one of the large steel fuel tanks, which was strong enough to withstand the pressure of steam from within. Then it was easy to connect the boiler with the motor by a pipe line. The complicated machinery of the rocket contained sufficient useful parts which could be detached.

Hope arose when Anderl, after ten hours of strenuous labor, declared that he had nearly finished but must make a test of the newly constructed steam turbine to see if it would really work.

The slight amount of gravitational influence made it much easier to bring the cumbersome machine out through the vault. A tackle, hastily constructed of rollers and ropes, took the place of a crane, and soon the turbine, coupled with the dynamo, stood on the base which had been prepared for it next to the boiler.

It was not so easy to procure water. There were several pools in the vicinity; yet, when Tommy attempted to carry a bucket of the precious liquid to the base of their operations, he would be driven to the point of distraction to find that it had evaporated or frozen, or both, on the way. Their only recourse was to carry the boiler to the pool to fill it. Then if the refractory water froze in the process of transportation, the concave mirrors could easily melt the ice inside it.

This done, Hardt adjusted the mirrors, connected the steam pipe and tightened the valve. The men, enveloped in their pneumatic suits, with only telephone communication between them, awaited the coming events in breathless expectation. It was obvious that their last hope of salvation rested upon the success of this experiment.

The steel container glistened brightly in the brilliant rays reflected upon it. In a few moments a thin white cloud of vapor issued from the valve, falling immediately to the ground in the form of frost. Hardt looked at Anderl with a significant smile, and continued to watch the manometer. The vapor became denser. Anderl opened the valve to the connecting pipe and the vapor streamed into the turbine. No sound was audible through the protecting suits, but the watchers saw the turbine gradually begin to turn.

"It works!" cried Tommy excitedly.

Anderl shook his head.

"The motor is idling, now," he said. "We can't tell how it will work under full steam."

He watched the machine closely for a few moments. Suddenly there was a gush of white steam; the turbine slowed down and finally stopped.

"Is it broken?" inquired Dr. Hardt.

Hardt turned the valve to the connecting pipe.

"The pipe is cracked," he said. "We must attach a larger one."

"Is that possible?"

"Somewhere in the ship I think we shall be able to find a piece for the purpose. Anyway, we can't expect too much from the first trial. It went better than I dared hope. With a few more hours of tinkering Anderl will have it working perfectly."

"Then we are saved?"

"That's a little too much to predict at present. In any event, we have motor power and an electric current. The next question is how to conduct the current into water to decompose it."

"That ought not to be so difficult," replied Dr. Hardt. "A larger water container for introducing the current, and gas pipes connecting with the tanks "

"There must be at least two containers with a connecting pipe," continued the engineer, Hone in which the current produces oxygen at the entrance point, and the other in which it produces hydrogen at the exit point. The two gases must be formed separately, for if they should combine they would form enough oxyhydrogen gas to explode at the slightest provocation and tear the whole business to pieces."

"Isn't that the kind of gas you want?"

"Yes."

"Then why are you still in doubt?"

"I do not doubt that we can produce hydrogen and oxygen, though the quantity is still undetermined. But even if we should produce unlimited quantities which would completely fill our tanks, there would be a question as to whether we could rise from the moon and make a smooth landing on earth."

"I don't see why," said Dr. Hardt in a disgruntled tone. "The tanks cannot be more than full."

"Oh, yes, they can," replied his nephew with a smile. "They can and must be more than full."

"Nonsense!" rudely contradicted Dr. Hardt. HI wish you were right, but listen! Not alone volume of fuel is necessary for the operation of the rocket, but also percentage of chemical energy, or its quantity according to weight. As you know, gases have no definite volume. A cubic meter may contain grams or kilograms according to pressure. The mere fact that our tanks are full means nothing. Not only must we fill the tanks with gas, but we must compress it, possibly to the point of liquefaction. Only then can the tanks hold a sufficient quantity."

"Excuse me, Hans!" replied the Doctor. "You are right. The gas must be pumped into the tanks."

"That would be easy if we were in our workshop in Friedrichshafen instead of on the moon. But everything is lacking here. Our pumps are not strong enough for the purpose, aside from the difficulty of mounting them. The only thing we can do is to produce the gas in an air-tight system of boiler, pipes and tank. It will then compress itself through limitation of space—but not if the pressure cracks some part of the apparatus."

"The tanks?"

"No, not those, for they are built to withstand high pressure. I am afraid the long connecting pipes, and more probably the comparatively weak joints, will give way long before the pressure is strong enough. Then we should have to begin all over again."

Meanwhile the two men walked around the spaceship, which gave the impression of some gigantic, prehistoric animal in the midst of the weird, fantastic landscape.

Once again Hardt tested the newly repaired leak. "That will hold as good as new!" he declared.

"Hans," said his uncle hesitatingly, "I have an idea. Please don't laugh at it."

"Out with it! The smallest thing may save the day for us."

"Supposing that, instead of trying to decompose the water in a boiler, you accomplish the process by introducing it directly into the *Wieland* tanks. In that way you would avoid any weak points. What do you think?"

Hardt stared at the speaker in amazement.

Then, involuntarily, he leapt into the air. "Uncle Alex!" he shouted. "You've got it!" Without further ado, he worked out his plan.

"The tanks, half filled with water, connected by pipes at the bottom; in one the anode, in the other the cathode; the gases, generated on the spot, automatically compress as they fill the tanks; at the bottom a manometer and a valve from which issues water as soon as the pressure has reached sufficient strength. It works, Uncle Alex! I would kiss you if I could through these helmets!"

It was a matter of some excitement that the Doctor had found the key to a problem in technical construction which had baffled even the chief engineer. Even Anderl's accomplishment was cast in the shade, and Dr. Hardt was the hero of the day.

Hardt promptly set to work at conducting the isolated electrodes into the tanks and setting up valves, after which everyone except Anderl, who was still working on the turbine, was instructed to carry water by means of the steel containers.

Fortunately the sun was shining on the black side of the ship, so that there was no danger from excess cold. After two hours of hard work the tanks were filled; Anderl had finished repairing the motor, and the incredible was accomplished.

The machine worked. The steam produced by the converged sun rays drove the turbine, and this in turn produced an electric current in the interior of the rocket.

But Anderl discovered to his alarm that the dynamo went dead. The four weary men were struck with dismay.

Suddenly Hardt laughed. "Of course!" he cried with nervous gayety. "How could we forget that water here is chemically pure, and pure water does not conduct a current. Quick, Mr. Bighead, bring all the salt you can find and put it in the tanks. We shall have to do without salt in our food!"

It took the salt some time to dissolve. Finally the indicator on the ammeter began to rise; bubbles of gas in unbroken succession blew into the tanks: they were of oxygen and hydrogen, the precious material which meant rescue.

The travelers had been on the moon for more than twenty-four hours, twenty-four hours of great strain and fatigue. Now came a period of calm—almost too much calm! Once started, their machine continued automatically to work and needed no other attention than a regular adjusting of the mirrors according to the slow progress of the sun, and an occasional checking of the imperceptibly rising pressure in the tanks. The sun would be with them for the equivalent of eight more days, and according to the quantity of fuel produced in the first eight hours of operation their tanks would be sufficiently full within that time for a return to earth, provided there were no superfluous weight and their fuel were of the proper quality.

A regular guard was established at the machine, which was under the constant vigilance of one man of the four. The remaining three could sleep or do anything they pleased. Hardt prohibited flights into the neighboring vicinity for the sake of conserving their supply of liquid air. Two exploring expeditions were agreed upon. When the sun reached the zenith, they would attempt to enter the deep funnel which they had discovered among the conical mountains. Later they would undertake the ascent of the circular mountain range in order to get a view of the moon's surface beyond the Triesnecker crater.

For the present, however, there was nothing to do, and their isolation, with their restricted space in the interior of the *Wieland* grew wearisome to the restless travelers. Dr. Hardt had carefully inspected everything that was to be seen from the ship. Tommy's manuscripts were piled high, and, rack his brain as he would, he could think of nothing more about which to write articles. Hardt and Anderl complained tha t there was nothing more to repair in the whole *Wieland*. With the lure of the sunny landscape before them, they felt as though they were imprisoned, and longed for some change in their situation.

"It's a pity," mused Dr. Hardt, "that that intriguing satellite didn't fall with us. It would give us material for weeks of research, for it hides more wonders than all the tombs of the Incas and the Pharaohs. We were stupid not to take something away with us from such a quantity of cosmic treasures."

"Excuse me, Doctor," retorted Tommy. "Do you include me in the category of nothing?"

"I didn't mean that at all," protested the Doctor, with a smile.

"You were the most valuable discovery ever made on that cosmic fragment. But you must admit, your worthy person does not offer a rich field for the discovery of primeval relics.".

"Would you be willing, Uncle Alex," said Hardt, "to tell us about what you found on the satellite? Unless I am mistaken, you have come to some conclusion about this mysterious body."

"Well, the time we spent there was too short and our explorations too superficial for anyone to venture a definite opinion about it. One thing, however, is certain. It has been the habitat of human beings, for the forces of nature neither create images nor write symbols, nor do they build ships."

"Do you mean a spaceship, in competition with us?" asked Tommy, with sudden interest.

"Even if the thing had really been a spaceship, we should need to fear competition no more than the League of Nations should fear Alexander the Great. The men who lived on this satellite belong to a race which disappeared more than twelve thousand years ago, and with them a culture which, in its perfection, has not been surpassed to this day.

"Whereas discoveries on earth have all been fragmentary, the silent, icy Universe has preserved for us a remnant of the dim, mythical, primeval ages. Man had first to penetrate the abysses of the Universe before completing his knowledge of his own youth, and to learn about a catastrophe to mankind which, heretofore, has been calculated only from the collapse of the sixth continent-the end of Atlantis."

Dr. Hardt sank into silent meditation.

"Tell us about it!" came three voices in unison.

"It can be no more than an hypothesis," he said, "which the discovery of the satellite makes more of a certainty. You know that no explorer likes to tell about things whose existence he cannot authenticate. If we had only had time to take impressions of the inscriptions, to examine the material more carefully, and to study the formations, then..."

"No excuses, Uncle Alex!" said Hardt. "You know more than you are admitting, and for the gaps in your knowledge you have theories. So let's have it! Give us a glimpse into the history of mankind."

The Doctor could refuse no longer, so he began.

XXVIII
EARTH'S
TRANSFORMATION

O NCE upon a time, where to-day the waves of the Atlantic moan their eternal dirge, there was a great insular group, extending from the Azores to Central America. The largest of these islands, the mythical island of Poseidon, mentioned by wise Solomon in ancient Egyptian sources, lay west of the Canary Islands. Among its hills was situated Thula of the golden gates, ancestral seat of the ruler of Atlantis.

"It was a golden era for mankind. The perpendicular position of the earth's axis brought about a climate that was like perpetual spring. There was no perceptible difference between the seasons; no harsh winter interrupted the ripening of nature's products; plants and fruits grew in extravagant abundance, sufficient for all men. The sun blessed the land in the daytime; but at night it was very dark, for as yet there was no moon. Men were much more closely allied to nature than they are to-day. They ruled over the secret forces of nature, not through their knowledge of science but through the impulse of their being: as the snake attracts the mouse by its hypnotic stare; as the bee seeks and protects its kingdom; in unconscious unity with the earth; by instinctive right.

"Thousands of years passed thus. Then man began to think, and to use his control over nature toward the end of having plants and animals serve him and procuring a surfeit of self-gratification. The snorting prairie horse was tamed to his service; the woolly mountain sheep was captured and deprived of its freedom; the gentle cat was reduced to a plaything. Wild-growing plants and fruits would no longer suffice him; he must transplant them, graft them onto each other, and confine them in narrow space, until finally there was cultivated a vine from slender, creeping, sun-steeped mountain plants, whose ripe grapes yielded an intoxicating juice.

"More and more man became aware of his power over nature, and eventually he attempted to humble men of inferior knowledge. His growing intellect impelled him to store up food and fuel in provision for times of less abundance. With the loss of his inner unity with nature, his understanding had to create a new sense of values, and new inventions to insure the continuation of his race and the satisfaction of his growing needs. As the power of understanding, however, developed unevenly among men, the mode of living of individual man gave varying manifestations. Thus originated the sense of possession. With possession came envy, ill-will and discord. No longer did men live beside one another, carefree, unenvious, in primitive harmony; but harmony had to be supported with laws, permitting or prohibiting, laws determining what was good or bad. As the restriction of laws always produces resistance, a central power had to be established for the purpose of forcing obedience to laws. Thus originated the king.

"The more men learned how to reason, the more their primitive capacities dwindled. They exulted in their cleverness and did not heed the passing of their primitive power. Only a few had retained their power over nature, and the man of knowledge regarded as miracles the accomplishments of these few, unaware that he himself had originally the same capacity. He retained a feeling of incompleteness in his being, and regarded with shy veneration the miraculous deeds of the 'enlightened' ones, which he could no longer grasp with his understanding. Thus came into being the priest.

"The budding intellect of man, together with the remains of his degenerating primitive power and inherent strength, combined with nature's opulence, brought into existence a culture and civilization which were the starting point of all cultures of the world—Atlantis!"

Dr. Hardt paused to fill his pipe, and then went on with his narration:

"The last ruler in the City of the Golden Gates on the island of Poseidon was a nature-worshiping king whom the Mayas in their myths called Botchica. Sincere and free from avarice, he attempted to preserve the remnant of that occult, primitive power. As an outward symbol of it, he carried at all official functions a ruler's staff of ebony and gold, adorned at one end with an obsidian, one of those dark, glassy stones which fell from a meteor. This stone bore an engraved symbol—a cross and a circle—the holy symbol of life and of the waning powers of nature."

"I remember seeing such a symbol in the decayed satellite," interrupted Hans Hardt.

"Yes, one specimen showed the head of a man bearing this symbol on his forehead," confirmed his uncle, and he continued:

"Whether any occult power really inhabited the stone remains a question. The people of Thula, however, considered that the stone held a demon whose power was under the sway of the stone's possessor. Having confidence in this demon's power, the strong island inhabitants began to make extended raids into the continents. The uncouth barbarians in the countries bordering the central sea were conquered. The armed hand of the haughty nation reached out, ever farther, over the earth, and there arose a kingdom on which the sun never set.

"The treasures of the world were brought together in Thula, the Golden City. Commerce flourished, and the island harbor swarmed with ships. The inhabitants of Atlantis indulged in extravagant drinking and reveling, while the conquered people starved in the chains of servitude. The world was oppressed by this plundering island people.

"Botchica, influenced by the pleadings of his subjects, had for some time experienced a change of heart. He called upon the pleasure-mad people to return to the purity and the simplicity of a self-sufficient life; but to no avail. A mania for blood and gold had seized the rulers of Atlantis. They no longer respected the mandates of the king, but rose up in arms against the ancient dynasty. Under leadership of the field generals, a rebellion was instigated; and the beautiful young queen, Huitaca, second wife of Botchica and last queen of Atlantis, was a fanatical accomplice of this rebellion.

"Botchica realized that trouble was brewing.

Had he possessed astrological knowledge through which he could have foreseen the approaching catastrophe, or had he perceived it through his nature-worshiping instinct—who knows? In any event, the warning voice of king and priest fell on deaf ears.

"Very quietly he set to work to rescue the culture of Thula. He sent messages throughout the world, peaceful proclamations of the knowledge and power of Atlantis. His son, Quetzalcoatl, departed westward into the country of present-day Central America, and taught the red children of Zeus how to build stone temples and houses. The daughter, Batschue, went eastward to the banks of the Nile, and, as Icim, or Isis, founded the kingdom of the Pharaohs. Messengers penetrated even distant Mongolia where, as enlightened sons of the gods, they spread their knowledge and culture.

"Wherever culture exists to-day, it originated with the colonizers of Atlantis. Small wonder that in the virgin forests of Mexico the same type of pyramid construction shot skyward as on the Nile; that the fauna and flora of Africa and America are so strangely similar; that the seedless banana, which can be transplanted only by slips or roots, grows in widely separated regions. The banana came out of Atlantis to Africa and America.

"What would our present culture be if some other than the farseeing Botchica had headed this plundering nation, doomed to destruction!

"Time flowed on into the sea of eternity. The people of the central sea united against the oppression of Atlantis. For decades they worked secretly on the preparation of a great fleet, which sailed out upon the sea through the Pillars of Hercules on its way to the glittering, arrogant city. The sea was covered with the ships of the ancient Hellenes.

"A battle was imminent. In Atlantis, the leaders of the fleet and of the army counseled King Botchica to use his power to destroy the oncoming enemy fleet with lightning and hail. After a

167

moment's hesitation, he refused. He could not use a power bestowed upon him by the gods for the destruction of man.

"At that the revolution broke out, with the beautiful young Queen Huitaca at its head. In a wild lust for power, she crept into the king's specious sleeping chamber in the stillness of the night, and broke from his staff the demoniacal moonstone. She then appeared before the people of Thula. Rejoicing, they crowded about the woman, raised her high on the throne, and sank into the dust before the new sovereign of the world.

"Huitaca's eyes glittered with the intoxication of her power. She raised the stone high over her head. 'Death to the enemy' ran the cry through the streets of Thula. The queen's pale lips twitched. With spasmodic gestures she swore to the spirits of nature that she would destroy the approaching enemy. The people were in a frenzy of joy. Suddenly the sky grew black; dark clouds in the north gave forth the sound of thunder; the storm burst in great fury. 'Death to the enemy!'

"Meanwhile Botchica, stricken with grief, stood on his observation post, the summit of a great pyramid at the edge of the city. The noise of the masses could scarcely reach the all-knowing, at this height. The grim catastrophe, which he had already foreseen, had arrived at last.

"Night came, and with it, horror! A star flamed up in the sky, gleaming ever more brightly. It rounded out into a glowing disc. It was the planet Luna, our moon! You know better than I, Hans, how it came, its course around the sun having gradually approached, through thousands of decades, the course of the larger, more slothful earth. On this night, Luna was falling as a sacrifice to the earth. Thrown out of its course in the realm of the sun, it drew nearer at frantic speed, drawn by the more mighty sister, lowered to the position of satellite of the earth.

"Like a glowing dragon, the moon rushed down out of space, in an elliptical path. It came quite near, so that its great red disc seemed to touch the earth, rushed back again, returned. This may have lasted for thousands of years, until the moon's course rounded out to its present path.

"The first approach brought the catastrophe.

"The moon's surface burst under the power of the earth's attraction. Water gushed forth from under the ice, vaporized in space and trailed out like the tail of a comet behind the speeding planet. The earth, too, felt the attraction of its new companion. The waters of the seas were drawn together and spread in gigantic spring tides from the poles to the equator.

"While the entranced people of Thula were under the spell of Huitaca, the calamity broke loose. Far to the north rose a perpendicular wall of towering water, destroying everything in its path. A wild hurricane tore down houses and twisted trees like straws. Mountains 'quaked; the suffering earth was rent asunder.

"Screaming with horror, the people scattered. They crept through the ruins of their dwellings. The storm was calm for a second; then the wall of water rushed over the city and submerged it. The last traces of man disappeared as the hissing, boiling waves pressed forward over the land.

"The great sea proceeded onward, with little resistance, south toward the equator. Mountains of foaming waves marked the location of the former flourishing Atlantis."

The narrator became silent.

"That's mighty interesting," remarked Tommy Bighead. "I hope those people in Atlantis had decent newspapers. Pardon my asking, but how do you know all this?"

Dr. Hardt smiled.

"From the myths and fables of various peoples. How terrible must have been this cataclysm of nature that it could live on for thousands of years, undimmed, in the minds of men, even to the present day. Through those thousands of years, the fables have taken various forms, according to the living conditions of the races. In later times the incidents have been confused and adapted to surroundings. The original story, however, upon which all these manifold versions are based, has remained unchanged."

"And how," asked Hans Hardt, "do you connect our moon's satellite with the destruction of Atlantis?"

Dr. Hardt studied the palms of his hands while he reflected.

Suddenly he looked up at his . nephew and said: "If the floor of the ocean cracked under the force of the mighty waves, if water penetrated the crevices and simmered in the burning interior of the earth, is it not conceivable that from this mingling of fire and water resulted a great undersea explosion which flung earth and water high into the infinite distance!"

"Certainly! If this eruption were forcible enough to impart a speed of seven and a half miles a second to the individual masses, and if these fragments were able to escape the perpetual attraction of the earth. Much of the mass must have landed in the open Universe. With the high speed through the lower air strata, the greater part of the hurtling masses must have been ground to dust by the air resistance and burned by the friction. It was different with our *Wieland*. We traveled through the thick layers of air at a comparatively low speed, and reached our true cosmic speed only beyond the air strata."

"Do you consider it entirely out of the question that at least a few of the fragments from the explosion broke through the air circle?'"

"Oh, that is quite conceivable. Heavy masses overcome air resistance better than light ones. Some of the larger individual fragments may have flown out into the Universe and escaped the earth."

"Then I do not need to cast aside my hypothesis. Incidentally, I believe that this mysterious satellite of the moon is nothing more than a fragment from that catapulting mass.

"It is evident that Atlantis possessed good ships, perfectly equipped and as strong as our submarines of to-day. What is more natural than that the despairing inhabitants of Thula sought safety in such boats from the onrushing flood. The boats may have been cast by the explosion into the Universe with no possibility of return. Perhaps it was the remains of the guilty Queen Huitaca's boat that we found in space, the last silent and eloquent testimonial of mankind's great tragedy, the drama of guilt and sin.

There was complete silence for a time. The tragic story of the dim past had deeply moved the listeners. Even Tommy Bighead, the ever-loquacious reporter, gazed out of the window, deep in thought, at the sky through which Huitaca's icy ghost had circled for twelve thousand years, a grim symbol of expiated guilt.

"The waves of the Atlantic now move restlessly over the abode where, once upon a time,, primeval man was surrounded with splendor and brilliance; and ships' keels glide high over the sunken, ancient city on the bottom of the sea."

XXIV
THE EXPLORATION
OF THE CRATER

THE fourth day after landing on the moon, Hardt, his uncle and Anderi set out to explore the deep, funnel-like crater among the conical mountains. They had equipped themselves with a supply of oxygen, ropes and makeshift staffs for traveling over the ice. It was useless to take food, as the helmets of their suits prohibited eating.

Tommy Bighead, to his intense disappointment, was left behind to watch the motor apparatus. All his pleading was in vain.

"One of us must remain with the *Wieland* Mr. Bighead," said Hardt, "and you are the only one with physical injury."

"I am as strong as an ox," insisted Tommy. "What does a little scratch on my hand amount to? Why, I could tackle a lion!"

"There will be little opportunity for that," replied Hardt in some amusement. "On the next expedition which we will make to the ridge of the mountains, you will be one of the party. To-day, however, I must ask you to serve as watchman."

Tommy had to resign himself. His eyes narrowed as he glanced at the favored Anderl, and the recently established peaceful relationship between the former antagonists was again in danger.

"You know, Mr. Bighead," said Hardt placatingly, as he observed Tommy's look of animosity, "if the manufacture of our motor power should meet any interruption, certain death would be our fate. You must remember the great responsibility resting upon you during our absence."

Tommy had secretly entertained some idea of slipping out, but touched by the commander's serious tone, and impressed by the importance of his task, he became reconciled. He made himself comfortable in the observation cabin and through the telescope watched the movements of the three grotesque figures, proceeding in long strides over the glittering ice. They receded into the distance until finally they were swallowed up in the deep shadows cast by the conical mountains.

The sun beat down on the bored and solitary Tommy. He began to wander aimlessly through the ship's interior. In the storeroom he unearthed a box of Havana cigars, and presently his gloom was dispelled in drifting blue clouds of smoke.

Meanwhile the three explorers had reached the edge of the crater. Dr. Hardt shuddered as he looked down the yawning abyss. The perpendicular walls of ice disappeared far below into a seething, bluish vapor which filled the whole basin.

"That looks as if this volcano intended to break forth at any moment," remarked Anderl, slightly apprehensive.

"You are wrong in considering this funnel a volcanic crater," replied Hardt. "There no longer is such a thing on this dead, icy moon."

"Yes, the inapt term 'crater' gives a wrong impression," commented Dr. Hardt. "It would be well to retain the true meaning of the Greek 'krater' which means nothing more than a beaker."

"What are those clouds of smoke, then?" inquired Anderl, pointing to the depths.

"Vapor. The air in the funnel is apparently denser than it is up here, and for that reason it is warmer in the funnel. Under the perpendicular rays of the sun, the melted ice gives off a vapor which, on reaching thinner air, freezes into fine needles of ice that fall to the ground by their weight. Thus there is a constantly circulating moisture produced by the sun, very much as is the case on earth. We need have no fear of these moving mists. Our suits protect us from all gases, and the vapor is far from hot. So let's enter!"

The three men attached themselves to each other by strong ropes and began the descent. The Doctor was the first to swing over the edge of the funnel. His nephew followed at a short distance, and Anderl brought up the rear. As the strongest and most experienced of the three climbers, to him fell the responsibility of holding the rope should his companions miss their footing.

The ice walls were cleft and indented with so many ridges that, despite their steepness, they offered no serious difficulties. Had Dr. Hardt been in possession of his earthly weight, he might have proved troublesome in his lack of experience. Each man weighed scarcely thirty pounds, however, outfit included, and in case of a fall would land in the depths with much less force than on earth, or would perhaps be able to find a new foothold before reaching the bottom.

They descended for about six hundred and fifty feet, whereupon minute icicles began to form on their rubber suits, due to the warmth inside, and before long, the shapeless, balloon-like figures took on the appearance of living snowmen.

The walls became damp and slippery; the mist grew denser; and finally the explorers paused at the verge of a dull, hazy obscurity which made continued progress highly dangerous. Hardt debated as to whether it would be advisable to return. But his uncle protested. "We can't be far from the bottom now. Why turn back for such a short distance!"

The expedition continued. Suddenly the Doctor stopped on a projecting platform and felt of the ice. "Come here, Hans," he called through the telephone. "We seem to have reached a bit of real ground."

Hardt hastened to the spot. "There's not a doubt," he agreed. "It is hard rock, a mass of rock which has pushed through the ice. It looks like gray slate."

"It looks to me more like iron ore. This is getting interesting. We must investigate further."

Bare spots became more frequent; ice was less in evidence; and water gurgled from all directions.

After another fifteen minutes, they had reached the crater's bottom. As far as they could determine through the dense mist, the ground was covered with an irregular mass of rocks, chunks of ice and bubbling pools of water.

The now useless ropes were laid aside. Anderl sprang from rock to rock in childish glee. Dr. Hardt diligently collected mineral specimens in a bag which he had fastened about his waist. Hans gazed meditatively into the dimly luminous vapor which shut off his view from the edge of the crater.

"It must have been a gigantic meteor that made this hole in the moon," he said, after some deliberation.

"Well, such meteors land on earth, too," replied the Doctor, still collecting his specimens. "As far as is known, the largest of these fragments fell into the Siberian province, Jenisseisk, in August, 1905. It crashed with a fearful noise and bored its way through fifty-two feet of solid earth. Even so, the tunnel left by this cosmic torpedo was discovered only a few years ago; for the native inhabitants of the place, in superstitious fear, had kept the secret hidden."

Dr. Hardt stopped suddenly, as though he had come across some unexpected discovery.

"What's the matter. Uncle Alex?" inquired Hardt.

"Look! Look!"

Involuntarily he lowered his voice, though no sound could come out of his helmet. "These dark spots are plant life; broad, fern-like weeds, stunted in their development..."

"I expected to find some sort of plant life here," calmly answered Hardt.

"Something has just moved among the leaves. There it is again..." Dr. Hardt advanced a few steps in his excitement.

"Stop! Stay where you are!" commanded Hardt abruptly, noticing the movement at the same instant. "We can talk as much as we like, for no sound can go outside of our microphones. But don't anybody move!"

Again the plants wavered. Almost immediately a gleaming gray streak came toward the observers from the obscurity. It was a snake, something with life. The moon was not as dead as people thought. The strange, slimy reptile lay motionless for a time, very near the men. "It is an amphibian, like a proteus," whispered Dr. Hardt. "It is almost colorless, and has no eyes, as is the case with the grotto proteus, which lives in perpetual darkness in the subterranean caves of the Dalmatian mountains. Such a large proteus does not exist in our realm, however. This animal is almost two yards long."

As Dr. Hardt bent nearer to examine the large wormlike body, with short, finlike legs which gave it a ludicrous appearance, the reptile lifted up the fore part of its body, and with head waving from side to side, instinctively opened and closed its jaws.

"The beast must have a telepathic sense of our presence, despite its lack of vision," said Dr. Hardt, grasping his staff more firmly.

Simultaneously the proteus clapped its strong, pointed tail to the ground, and gave a sudden leap upward. Its undulating body flew through the mist in broad, spiral curves, and finally disappeared from the astounded gaze of the explorers.

"We should have caught that animal," exclaimed Dr. Hardt regretfully. "It would have made a splendid specimen for a zoological museum—a lunar proteus, discovered, captured, mounted, by Alexander Hardt—sounds well, doesn't it?"

Hardt looked around inquiringly. "Where is Anderl?" he inquired in concern. "His cable must be broken or he would have taken part in our conversation. Anderl!"

There was no reply.

"This basin is haunted," said Dr. Hardt, trying to appear calm, "but I don't think these salamanders can be dangerous, especially to a man of Anderl's size."

"You are probably right. Uncle Alex. But our protection depends upon our suits remaining intact. If they are damaged or torn in any way, even our comparatively great strength cannot keep us from suffocation and our veins from bursting through diminished pressure."

"I am afraid Anderl is relying too greatly upon his muscular strength and forgetting to be cautious."

Unfortunately the explorers had not brought a barometer with which to determine the pressure prevailing in the crater. In any case, it was far from strong enough for any human being without the aid of artificial respiration.

"Let's start looking for him!" exclaimed Dr. Hardt, without even having detached a clump of plants for specimens. "All we need to do is to follow the cable and we shall find him."

The cable lay coiled on the ground, indicating the path Anderl had taken. Hardt picked up the cable, winding it as he proceeded. His uncle trudged along beside him. A hundred yards brought them to the end of the cable where Hardt found the brass plug. "Careless fellow," he muttered. "He loosened the connection of his own accord. He probably espied something interesting beyond the limit of the cable and freed himself."

With no possibility of seeing more than ten yards through the mist, and calls being of no avail, they could only wander at random through the crater. They went further and were stopped by a steep wall.

Then they decided to separate only so far as the cable would reach. Hardt turned to the right and stopped to survey the unexplored section. His uncle turned to the left. Their lightness made it easy to spring over blocks of ice and other obstacles. They spoke to each other frequently through the microphone to reassure themselves of continued communication. Several times Hardt stumbled on a block of ice which, in the misty vagueness, he mistook for Anderl.

All at once Hardt heard his uncle panting through the microphone, as though he were running. "What's the matter?" he asked tensely.

The answer came in horrified gasps. "There he is— Oh, terrible! Come quick! This is revolting! Those reptiles have gone mad!"

Hardt followed the cable in great leaps. He didn't bother to roll it up, and disconnected it in order to be less impeded. In twenty seconds he had reached his uncle's side, and gazed in horror at the gruesome spectacle which met his eyes.

In a field of rusty brown, leafy plants, groped Anderl. About his body were wound a dozen or so of the pale, slimy reptiles. Anderl was desperately struggling to free himself from the foul worms. He had already crushed some of the smaller ones against

177

his heavy helmet, but he was unable to overpower the mass of them. His movements were hampered by holding tightly with his left hand to a fold of his trousers.

The snakelike animals were already attacking Dr. Hardt, who was attempting to aid Anderl, and the former had enough to do to take care of himself.

Hardt reflected for a moment. He could not crush the animals with his knife or staff without endangering Anderl. What could he do? He cautiously approached the wriggling maze. Anderl raised his free hand in warning and pointed to the knee to which he was holding fast. The engineer was seized with alarm. He understood that Anderl's suit was torn, penetrated by the thorny tail of one of the salamanders, and Anderl was pressing the gap together so as to lose no air.

What now? If he entered the squirming mass, all would be lost. But how could he fight it?

He had no firearms, and if he had, they would do little good. Then came a sudden inspiration—oxygen! Quickly loosening the reserve tanks from their holder, he unscrewed the valve from one of the bottles. A thick vapor shot forth. With the cold resulting from the rapid vaporization of the liquid air, he hoped to be able to drive away the salamanders. The suits would be unaffected, as had been proven in the heatless Universe.

He directed the stream toward Anderl, who was most badly in need of help. The salamanders, sensing danger, erected their slimy bodies and seemed disposed to attack the new enemy. They did not come far, however. The hideous animals froze within a few seconds, and fell like rigid pieces of rope to the ground.

Anderl stood up and knocked off the stiff, lifeless forms of the salamanders. Dr. Hardt, too, was soon rid of his assailants.

"Cursed pests!" exclaimed Anderl when communication among the three men was again restored. "They intended to squeeze me to death. If they had been large earth snakes, I should have been crushed. But these moon beasts are not so powerful. It was the thorns! Pretty soon it would have been all up with me!"

"Let's get out of here!" exclaimed Hardt.

"They'll be coming to life again pretty soon, for if they can withstand the cold of night, they can't be dead."

Anderl limped, holding his knee.

"How large is the hole?" asked Hardt.

"No larger than a bullet hole. It was well that I noticed it, feeling the cold, before another hole was made, or it would have been good-by Anderl! It's queer how these soft, spongy animals have thorns hard enough to penetrate leather as if it were nothing. My finger is lame from having to hold this together."

"Don't let go of it, Anderl, under any circumstances. Come on! The salamanders will soon be moving!"

As rapidly as possible the men proceeded to the nearest wall. Anderl was helpless because of the hole in his suit. Hardt and his uncle slowly climbed upward, drawing Anderl after them. After some considerable difficulty they reached the ice zone.

They didn't need to be afraid of the salamanders here, and daylight shone about them. They halted in a covered passage.

"Now let's have a look, Anderl," said Hardt. "Perhaps we can mend the broken place."

He drew the fabric together and tied it with a cable wire. Then he cautiously released it and found that the knot would hold and prevent the leakage of air.

Anderl was now free to move, which was fortunate. In their battle with the reptilian animals, they had used so much oxygen that they must hasten in order to reach the *Wieland* before the remainder gave out. Anderl sprang along with the agile strength of a panther.

The Doctor remained behind to wrap up some bright object.

"For Heaven's sake, Uncle Alex, what have you there?" called his nephew.

"Do you think I am going to leave this crater empty-handed, just as I left the ship of Atlantis?" calmly retorted the archeologist, as he threw his pack on his back.

In fact, he was carrying a frozen proteus, an excellent specimen more than two yards long, and he was particularly careful that it should not be damaged during the return trip. It had lost considerable of its white color, transformed by the sunlight into blue-black and rusty-brown spots through the reaction of its sensitive skin to the light. Only the shaded surface remained colorless.

In the thinner and colder air, Anderl did not fear that the proteus would return to life.

In half an hour the explorers stood before the *Wieland.* Tommy was nowhere to be seen, and the windows of the observation cabin were clouded. Smoke filled the vault, pouring in from the inner valve, and on opening the inner door, Hardt found the cabin filled with the same dense smoke. He laid aside his helmet in some annoyance.

"Good evening, Mr. Hardt!" Tommy's voice came from an invisible source.

"Man, aren't you suffocated here?" called the engineer into the clouds of smoke. "This is worse than the crater." He opened an exhaust valve and set the fan in motion, which improved matters somewhat.

"No, I'm not suffocated," replied Tommy, puffing steadily on his cigar. "I've been very comfortable. Only it was lonesome, and I am glad you are back again."

"We have brought something remarkable back with us," said Dr. Hardt, entering at this moment, and removing his heavy outer garment. "It is a highly interesting specimen for a museum—a real lunar proteus. Wait till you see it!"

Eagerly he unwrapped his bundle.

"Lunar proteus? I don't know what that might be, but I see it is not a very appetizing dish."

The Doctor's great astonishment and recoil from his precious proteus caused a hearty roar of laughter. The animal had collapsed in the thin air outside of the crater, like a decayed rubber tube. The "specimen" had changed into an odorous, gelatinous, slimy mass of boneless viscera.

XXX
SHADOWS

THEIR remarkable adventures in the crater of the salamanders furnished the four lonely wanderers on the moon with abundant material for conversation during the next few days. Tommy Bighead felt increasingly regretful that he had not been on the scene.

"Your struggle with those beasts should have been photographed," he declared with his customary assertiveness. "As it is, we have no proof, and no one will believe the story."

"All the scientists in the world will shake their heads at the statement that there is life on the desolate moon," replied Hardt. He looked at his uncle for confirmation.

"Well," began the latter, "such a discovery is not entirely incredible. No one positively denies that the moon may have given shelter to life in past ages, as well as the earth, and that its surface may have held animals and forests as long as it could offer conditions favorable to the existence of life. As the moon lost its protective mantle of air, all forms of life had to withdraw into the deeper crater valleys, until finally only in the deepest holes could flora and fauna preserve themselves. There, in complete seclusion, they developed their own characteristic forms.

"I am convinced that the proteus is not the only inhabitant of the moon at present. Many years ago the American astronomer, Pickering, perceived in one of the moon craters brown, moving spots which he thought might be swarms of insects. Other forms may have been discovered in other craters. These individual centers of life have no connection with one another."

"Exactly so!" said Tommy pointedly. "The fate awaiting the inhabitant of a crater outside of his natural abode has been emphatically demonstrated in your 'splendid museum specimen.'"

"We should have preserved the proteus in closed alcohol containers," replied the Doctor gloomily. "If it had only left at least a skeleton! But the inconsiderate beast didn't have any bones."

"Well, you can look forward to what I shall bring you from our next expedition. Doctor," said Tommy arrogantly, as he slapped the scientist on the back in a condescending manner.

Tommy was out of luck, however. On the expedition to the circular range of mountains of which he was a member three days later, there was no sign of an adventure. The ascent of the mountain wall enclosing the plain offered no difficulties because of their light weight, though there was an immense altitude to reach. The particular depression among the mountains which they had set as their goal was at a height of 6,500 feet.

Once outside the Triesnecker crater, the view was impressive, to say the least. Below extended an ocean of glassy ice, masses of glittering mountain tops in desolate confusion, mingled with numerous dark crater ravines of various sizes, and greenish plains indented with ridges.

The powerful, penetrating light of the setting sun lay over it all, leaving deep shadows on the landscape. On the southern horizon arose the grotesque white masses of the circular Rhasticus mountains against the black depths of space, and high above them among the gleaming stars hung the lighted hemisphere of the distant earth. The attention of the three wanderers focused irresistibly upon it, and each one of the three felt the same longing:

"Will we ever tread its ground again, look upon the blooming of spring and upon blue skies, talk with other human beings?"

"I wish I could go fishing for blue shark on Lake Constance," said Anderl suddenly; and nobody laughed at this irrelevant remark, which was an expression of their own yearning for home.

Probably at this very moment on the dark side of the earth's

disc above them, men stood gazing upward at the shining full moon, just as Hans Hardt and his companions were gazing up at the distant earth. Their glances must have met somewhere in the Universe, full of man's insatiable desire: to go to the moon, and then to return home! And rest!

Tired and hungry, the wanderers returned to the ship fourteen hours later. Dr. Hardt, who had remained behind this time, had prepared a fine dinner. "A hangman's meal," he remarked, with a wry smile, ripping open the can of sardines. "Hereafter, we shall have to go without delicacies and be thankful that at least the zwieback is holding out."

The next day Hardt and his uncle performed some experiments with the minerals the scientist had brought with him out of the crater. A few pieces proved to be strongly radio-active, and when Dr. Hardt from the shadow of the crater wall concentrated the short-wave gamma rays of the Universe upon the stones, directing the reflections toward the Milky Way, he made the beginning of an important discovery.

Through the condensation of this mysterious radiation, which on earth is almost completely absorbed by the air and for that reason uneffective, the disintegration of the radiating matter was greatly accelerated.

"This experiment," declared Hardt, "is of primary significance for the spaceship of the future. If we could master the secret of disintegrating atoms, our proud *Wieland*, with her machine dependent upon the transformation of molecules, would be a mere plaything compared with electron rockets, emitting electrons with a speed equal to that of light. With such ether ships it would be a simple matter to go through space as far as our neighboring planets, Venus and Mars, and even to ringed Saturn."

For the time being, however, such fantastic plans for the future had to be held in abeyance. In the absence of equipment, they had to be content with improvised and unsatisfactory experiments.

The mountain shadows lengthened, and the wide shaded area at the foot of the great mountain wall spread. Almost imperceptibly it advanced across the wide region, and it was only a question of hours until it would reach the *Wieland*. Hardt could not permit that under any circumstances. The decomposed water in the tanks would freeze, with no possibility of direct sunlight to draw it off, and the ice would be inevitable and dangerous ballast. He, therefore, reluctantly decided to risk starting a day earlier than he had intended, and not wait for complete sunset.

He reckoned the height of the sun, whose rays were already slanting and were not radiating much heat. "We must start in four hours," he said, and gave instructions for the ship to be cleared.

Everything which could possibly be dispensed with was carried out into the open, including all kitchen utensils, the electric grill, pots, pans, dishes, chairs, tables, etc.

"We have nothing left but zwieback, and we can eat that from our hands," declared Dr. Hardt to the reporter, who had protested at these energetic measures.

The kitchen fixtures were followed by the cases from the supply room; empty oxygen bottles, reserve leather outfits, the toolchest; only the small first aid chest and a few absolutely necessary articles of clothing escaped the fate of remaining spoil to the moon night.

Hans Hardt experienced an almost physical pain when he began to dismount the costly optical instruments. They did not weigh in the balance, however, with the lives of four people.

Soon a veritable mountain of miscellaneous objects surrounded the *Wieland*, yet still more appeared. Blankets, superfluous hammocks and coils of rope were added to the heap.

Tommy Bighead carefully guarded his manuscripts. He stuffed all his pockets with notes in order to save them from the general destruction.

"Poor little bird!" exclaimed Anderl as he threw out the canary's cage. "It is a good thing that you are already dead. Otherwise, you would have to trust to this experiment!"

Hardt reckoned out the necessary amount of drinking water, food and oxygen. "Either the landing on earth will be accomplished in exactly four days, according to calculations, or else it will fail, and whether we suffocate, starve, or are dashed to pieces a few hours earlier or later, will be of little consequence. And so, get rid of everything unessential."

The process of storing up fuel went on, meantime, uninterrupted. It would continue so until the last minute, in order to have as great a supply of the precious gas as possible. Stinting in that respect would be nothing short of suicide.

The cleaning out process was finished half an hour before the time set for departure. The commander summoned all on board. "It is my duty," he said seriously, "to explain to you just what are our hopes of salvation."

The three comrades stood in uneasy silence about the engineer.

"In order to overcome the attraction of the moon," he began, "we need an impetus of a mile and a half a second. That is the least. But we can easily get away from the moon. The earth will draw us toward her of her own accord, and as soon as we have entered the gravitation limits, our speed will naturally increase until toward the end it will be seven miles a second. This speed must be checked by the counteracting effect of our explosive gas. For our return home, our fuel must have a driving force adequate for one and a half plus seven, and that makes eight and a half miles per second."

He turned to look at a gauge. The manometer on the tank showed a driving force of not quite six and a half miles per second. "In two days," he said, "our power would have increased to the necessary degree. But we can wait no longer. Look outside. The shadow lies already no more than two yards ahead of us. It is the icy herald of death by night on the moon."

"And that would be the end of writing columns for the Michigan Evening Post, wouldn't it!" said Tommy in perturbation.

"The prospects look darker than they really are," replied the engineer, in an effort to dispel the rising pessimism. "In the first place, we have lightened the ship a great deal. We can't estimate exactly how much, as we are unable to weigh the material left behind. In any event, the manometer on the tank is adjusted for normal conditions and reads ten per cent lower than it really is. Furthermore, we can take advantage of the retarding action of the dense atmosphere until our hull begins to melt; and then, as a last resort, we have our parachutes. I repeat that our landing on earth will be dangerous; but our attempt is not without possibilities, and there is no cause to feel discouraged."

Now Hans Hardt, once more at his post of command, instructed Anderl to disconnect the cables leading to the power station and to run off the undecomposed water from the tanks.

"How about the light motor?" inquired Dr. Hardt.

"That has to stay behind. We shall need neither light nor heat."

"But the motor," insisted Dr. Hardt. "That controls the flywheels governing our direction. Are we to leave that?"

"It has to be, Uncle Alex. We have no choice."

"Then we can't steer the *Wieland*. What shall we do?"

"I have thought of that. We shall be able to get along without any motor. And now get into your hammocks. Pressure is going to come on immediately, and none of us is accustomed to it at present."

Anderl returned, took off his pneumatic suit, and announced: "The *Wieland* is clear for the start!"

He then carefully closed both doors of the vault and lay down in his hammock.

The space travelers took a last look through the windows at the ice-covered crater valley which had harbored them for ten days and could have become their final resting place. Hardt turned on the current. The pumps hummed vigorously.

"Take a deep breath," he called and pushed the fuel lever. Simultaneously pressure was felt.

The *Wieland* glided aloft along the smooth, perpendicular wall against which it had leaned, shot above the icy, conical mountain and whizzed like a lurid flash of lightning out into space.

One minute later the cold death-dealing shadow crept over the cases, instruments and machines which had been left behind.

XXXI
HOMEWARD BOUND

THE exhausts of the *Wieland* functioned only a hundred seconds before the speed of a mile and a half was reached which would carry them away from lunar attraction. As soon as Hardt disconnected the fuel line after attaining the parabolic speed, the familiar condition of lightness instantly reappeared. Like a rock hurled into the air, the ship speeded out through the moon's magnetic limits. In six hours it had crossed the neutral zone, and from there, with gradually increasing speed, moved toward the earth under the powerful attraction of this huge planet, which was their home.

"We shall fall like this for seventy hours," explained Hardt, "without power or steering. The earth automatically takes care of that. During the entire period, we shall have nothing to. do but to ascertain from time to time the distance of the earth, by measuring the angles, and to watch the operation of the air generator. I propose that one of us stand guard in the control room while the other three sleep."

"To sleep eighteen hours out of twenty-four is an art worth learning," retorted Tommy Bighead.

Hardt laughed.

"The absence of gravity will assist you in this arduous task, Mr. Bighead. Just try it. The best thing for us to do is to sleep a lot. For one thing, a rested state will make more endurable the hardships of the landing to come; for another, a person needs less oxygen and less food when asleep than when awake."

They drew lots to decide the order of the watch.

Inasmuch as the moon, during the ten days' sojourn of the travelers upon it, had completed one third of its revolution around the earth, the *Wieland* was approaching the latter on its illuminated side. During the entire journey the travelers had before them the almost three-quarters lighted disc.

At the end of the second day after their departure from the moon, their home planet extended beneath them in such size that it looked like a huge, carefully made, globe atlas. The light areas were sharply distinct from the dark areas of water. The large mountain ranges were discernible to the naked eye.

Anderl sat at a window and passed the time by searching out the location of large cities. The edge of the shadow was now passing through the middle of Europe. Berlin was already in darkness, while the British Isles were still visible. With the one telescope that Hardt had left on board, he studied the summits of the Alps in order to discover Lake Constance. But increasing darkness concealed his home. He was just about to level his telescope on America, still in the splendor of the noon sun, when he noticed in the dark region of the Alps an area of light. He eagerly watched this spot. The light appeared, disappeared and reappeared—dimly, to be sure, but nevertheless, clearly perceptible.

The flashes of light were not of equal duration. Short flashes alternated with long flashes of almost a second. That surely was no coincidence. Anderl was filled with hope. Were these flashes Morse signals, and were they intended for the *Wieland*? Had they seen the approach of the spaceship?

While noting down the dots and dashes, he called his chief. This matter was much more important than sleep. His call aroused not only Hans Hardt, but also Dr. Hardt and Tommy. The four space travelers forthwith gathered in the observation cabin.

"The earth is signaling us!" announced Anderl without lifting his eyes from the telescope.

Tommy Bighead, as an outlet for his glee, staged an original negro dance in three dimensions. "We must answer," he shouted. "We can get through some press cablegrams. I'll bet they'll be on every newsstand in Detroit within an hour. Tommy Bighead's First

Report on Hans Hardt's Trip to the Moon'; 'The Living Meteor'; "Horrible Struggle for Life against the Moon-p-p-pr . . '" He choked.

"Take it easy, Mr. Bighead. Don't get so excited," said Hardt, who was himself half crazy with joy.

Dr. Hardt deciphered the signs which Anderl had noted.

"W-i-e-l-a-n-d; W-i-e-1-a-n-d . . ."

"That's certainly meant for us!" exclaimed Tommy.

"It is always the same word," grumbled Anderl. "Can't those nit-wits think of anything else to say?"

"That's enough to tell us that they have noticed our approach," replied Hardt. "Or do you expect them, Anderl, to signal the latest price of beer?"

"What observatory do you think is signaling?" inquired Dr. Hardt.

"Apparently Mr. Kamphenkel has set up all the reflectors he could find anywhere around Lake Constance, and has directed all those millions of candle powers of light toward us. It would be well if we could send them a message, but we have neither light nor reflectors."

For five minutes the light flashed out into space the word "*Wieland.*" Then other signals appeared.   Dr. Hardt diligently deciphered them:

"A-l-l o-b-s-e-r-v-a-t-o-r-i-e-s w-a-t-c-h-i-n-g a-l-l s-h-i-p-s n-o-t-i-f-i-e-d b-y w-i-r-e-l-e-s-s w-h-o-l-e e-a-r-t-h a-l-a-r-m-e-d f-i-n-d h-e-l-p i-n a-l-l s-t-a-t-e-s . . ."

This sentence was repeated until Central Europe had disappeared from the ship's range of vision.

Hans Hardt was much pleased at this report. "Very good," he said. "Kamphenkel has certainly done things right. We can't tell on what part of the earth we shall land, since we can no longer steer our rocket. It is, therefore, very reassuring to learn that they are ready to receive us in any part of the earth. Naturally, the large observatories will follow our course and report their observations to one another. If any relatives happen to be watching us, they will be able to calculate the approximate place of our landing in the last hours of the descent, and will quickly send us help: that is, in case we do not land in the Sahara Desert or in Greenland. That's one load off our minds. It's stupid that we have no means of reassuring Kamphenkel and thanking him."

"It is indeed unpleasant," agreed Tommy in his disappointment, and he took Anderl's place at the watch.

The next few hours passed without special event. The terrestrial globe increased in size against the dark background, and it was the moon now which curved into a silver, shining crescent.

When Dr. Hardt came to relieve Tommy, he was astonished at the threatening aspect of the .gigantic sphere, looming toward them. Its dimensions increased, and it rushed toward the *Wieland* like some monster of cosmic space. Before he had finished his watch, he awakened his nephew, who aroused instantly.

"What's the matter?" he asked quickly.

"We are very near the earth!" said the Doctor. "I think it is time to do something."

Hardt took his bearings with a rapid observation and measurement of the angle at which the earth appeared.

"We still have four hours before starting landing maneuvers," he said calmly, "but nevertheless, it is better to be prepared an hour or two ahead of time than a second too late."

The engineer remained at his post from now on. The Doctor showed no desire to sleep, and kept his nephew company.

"We are heading directly for the eastern side of the earth," said Hardt after a longer observation. "That is a good thing!"

"Why is that a good thing?"

"Because the end of our course will be parallel with the revolution of the earth and not against it. Our speed, relative to that of the earth's surface, is thus diminished by 2,275 feet a second. A saving of that many feet a second is not to be despised by the *Wieland*. She is almost a wreck."

"Where do you think we shall land?"

"That is still difficult to predict. Our course takes us a long way around the earth, and in so doing gradually approaches nearer the earth's surface. If necessary, the point at which our circular path would cut into the earth could be calculated. The earth, however, is revolving; and besides that, the retarding influence of the air is uncertain. At any rate, we shall remain in the northern hemisphere. More than that I cannot tell."

The earth was now so near that it no longer appeared like a planet hovering in space, but like their own terra firma, over which the spaceship flew at a tremendous height.

Hardt aroused the two sleeping men, and for the last time the crew prepared for maneuvers. They were faced with the most difficult part of the entire journey—landing with insufficient fuel.

XXXII
THE LANDING

THE next thing was to throw all rubberized suits overboard. "We don't need these any more," said Hardt, "and they will lighten the ship by three hundred pounds." The suits disappeared from sight.

The absence of the motor for operating the steering system was a serious drawback. The massive steering gear had to be moved by hand levers, and it took two men almost a quarter of an hour of strenuous labor to turn the exhaust end of the ship toward the eastern side of the earth.

"As soon as we have penetrated the outer air strata," explained Hardt reassuringly, "we shall not need the flywheels. Other means will be at our disposal."

Anderl being the strongest of the four men, remained on duty at the steering gear. The others took their places in the hammocks. Hardt allowed the ship to drop freely toward the earth for three minutes. Dr. Hardt ascertained by a hasty observation that the *Wieland* was just traveling in a southeasterly direction above the great snow-covered area of Alaska. Then he closed his eyes. The pressure was bearing down on his chest.

The pilot allowed the exhausts to work for one minute at an acceleration rate of 114 feet a second. Then he shut them off. At this first retardation, the ship's speed had been decreased by about 6,500 feet a second.

"We have now reached the so-called revolution speed," said Hardt. "There will be no possibility from now on of the *Wieland* being lost in outer space. She is circling the earth at an altitude of approximately five hundred miles, and would continue in this manner even if we had no more fuel."

This moment's relaxation in the landing maneuvers was employed in correcting the deflection of the exhausts from the direction of their course. The lengthwise axis of the ship was made parallel with the earth's surface, with the exhaust in front and the prow in the rear. During the time consumed in this operation, the ship had approached the east coast of America. The pilot turned on the fuel for a second attempt at stopping.

For two minutes the fiery streams belched forth from the ship and checked the speed to two and a half miles a second. The path of the rocket was in the form of an ellipse which curved gently down to the surface and promised to land them on the western coast of Europe.

Gravity was apparent now, even with the exhausts shut off, and a slight pressure opposing their fall held the occupants of the *Wieland* fast in their hammocks.

"We are in the thinner, upper strata of the atmosphere," replied Hardt to a question of Tommy's. "Our speed is decreased by the air resistance, even when our exhausts are silent. This accounts for the slight pressure."

"Good! In that event we can save our fuel!"

"We still have a supply sufficient for a mile and a half a second. For the moment, however, we are traveling at a speed of more than two miles a second. We must depend upon air pressure for the difference. Otherwise..." He interrupted himself and looked at the dials showing temperature.

"Yes, and then?" inquired Dr. Hardt. "If it doesn't do that, will our journey slowly die down in the air?"

"Yes, Uncle Alex. It is only a question of whether the ship will melt over our heads. The exterior has already a heat amounting to 302° Fahrenheit; and it is increasing. We have to check our speed again, because if we continue like this into the lower air strata, the *Wieland* will burn up like so much tinder."

"In doing so, will our course be downward toward the earth?"

"Naturally!"

"Oh, dear! Then we are going to fall into the sea! That's not such a pleasant prospect."

"It can't be helped, Uncle Alex. We may be thankful we are bringing our ship back, safe and sound."

In the third attempt, they lost 4,550 feet per second.

Tommy gave a deep sigh in his hammock. "I'm getting squeezed to a pulp in here. Will this last long?"

"No," curtly replied Hardt, and called Anderl.

"We don't need the steering flywheels any longer, Anderl," he said, with feigned composure. "The air is dense enough so that you can release the brakes."

The lad went immediately about his work. He worked slowly and certainly as though he were in a laboratory in Friedrichshafen. From the prow toward the rear was thrown a cable, with conical projections of lead like the scales on the tail of a dragon. These projections resisted the air, and the cable lashed in wide circles behind the ship, thus acting as a strong brake. Naturally it was a matter of seconds before the lead projections became red hot from the friction. Anderl pushed off the cable and new ones followed, glowed and disappeared. In this manner they reduced much of the *Wieland's* motion into whirlwinds and heat; and while the sheets of lead were offered as a sacrifice, the ship was protected from the terrible heat.

The ship kept true to its course, better than the flywheels could have held it. In three minutes the supply of braking material was exhausted, but the ship's speed had been appreciably slowed down, and its path was directed rather abruptly toward the Atlantic Ocean.

Meanwhile, Hardt had prepared the parachutes for use and let down the rope ladders, in which Tommy helped with mixed feelings.

"Now we are ready!" called the engineer, no longer able to hide his feverish excitement. "Everyone get into the capsule of the parachutes, and be quick about it!"

"And you, Hans?" Dr. Hardt was trembling with concern for his nephew.

"No questions!" replied Hardt. "I will follow as soon as the exhausts work. All ready?"

"All ready," answered Anderl's quavering voice.

"Then throw out all the remaining fuel!" ordered the engineer through compressed teeth. At the same moment he pulled the fuel lever. For the last time the naming gas spit forth from the *Wieland*'s exhausts, trailing out from the rear like the tail of a comet, making a sheath of fire around the smooth metal body of the rocket.

When Hardt had convinced himself that the exhausts were working properly, he left the control room and climbed heavily up the ladder. The pressure was now so great that he would not have succeeded in reaching the parachute capsule, had not Anderl assisted him. Crowded closely together, the four heavily-breathing men cowered in the small round space. Anderl closed the small port window through which entered very little light from the control room.

The roar of the exhaust pipes was clearly audible, a sign that the ship was flying through thick layers of air, causing reverberations. If the *Wieland* had possessed wings, it could have descended like an ordinary airplane, in a smooth glide.

"As soon as the exhausts stop, Anderl," panted Hardt, "tear the cord. Do you understand?"

"Certainly, Mr. Hardt!"

This cord passed through a hole in the capsule to one of the switches built on the front of the rocket. Anderl was holding it in his hand. In silence they listened to the sound coming from below. Seconds seemed like hours.

"Perhaps the fuel will last, after all," softly ventured Dr. Hardt.

"No, decidedly not!" replied the engineer harshly. And in his voice deep pain was evident. "The *Wieland* is lost!"

"What?" said Tommy Bighead. "The *Wieland* lost? Why didn't you tell me that before? My manuscripts! They are still in the sleeping cabin. Stop? Stop? I must get them."

Anderl grumbled as he started to open the door leading below.

"Be quiet!" thundered Hardt. "Are you crazy? Not a sound, or I will shoot you on the spot!"

The reporter halted, in utter astonishment. Hardt regretted

his unwarranted anger, and was almost ashamed of his outbreak. The knowledge that his beloved ship was now hopelessly lost put him, the builder and successful pilot through all cosmic perils, into an apathy of despair. Presently, however, he felt sorry for the disconsolate American. What was more natural than that Tommy should consider his manuscripts more valuable than the spaceship? It was certainly greatly in his favor that he thought more of his profession at the present moment than of the danger to his life.

Hardt was beginning to explain his behavior, but the words died before utterance. The exhaust pipes were silent; the tanks were empty.

Anderl quickly pulled the cord. The whole front of the spaceship opened wide, and the capsule was flooded with daylight. A strong headwind seized the folded parachutes and inflated them. The connecting ropes broke loose, and with a sharp lunge the parachutes lifted the four men in the safety capsule out of the path of the falling ship.

Hardt gazed sadly down through a window below. Far beneath them the *Wieland* had struck the foaming waves and disappeared forever. Hans Hardt's spaceship was gone!

The capsule, too, fell so rapidly that the lowest of the three parachutes burst under the air pressure; but the other two held firm and checked the abruptness of the fall. As lightly as a soap bubble it wafted down through the last hundred yards to the sea. It landed on the water with a splash, sank down for a couple of yards, and reappeared. Hollow and completely round, it floated bobbing like a cork over the waves.' In close proximity the huge parachutes danced along in the brisk wind, until they became wet through and floated like yellow bubbles on the surface of the water.

And so, the space travelers had arrived safe and sound on the surface of the earth. They had returned home from distant planets; but they came empty-handed except for their lives.

XXXIII
CONCLUSION

THE Italian de luxe steamer, *Cleopatra*, on its route from Rio de Janeiro to the Canary Islands, had just crossed 20 degrees Latitude when the watch announced: "Airship in sight!"

The encounter of a steamer and an airship on the high seas was nothing out of the ordinary;

but the bored passengers welcomed the most insignificant occurrence to relieve the monotony of the long sea voyage. Glasses were taken out; a hundred pairs of eyes peered to the northeast where, high above the horizon, a dark spot had become visible against the sky.

The captain on the bridge did not take the marine glasses from his eyes.

"Is it a mailplane from the Azores line?" inquired the first officer.

"I don't think so. It is not on the proper course. Let us wait. Have the wireless operator warned to be in readiness."

At that moment the wireless operator appeared on the bridge.

"What was that strange message we picked up yesterday morning?"

The man drew a paper from his pocket and read:

"To all ships on the high seas. Within the next forty-eight hours is awaited the return of the German spaceship, the *Wieland*, from the moon. Since it is unknown on what part of the earth the rocket will alight, will all ships post special watches and hasten to the aid of the spaceship as soon as it is sighted? The International Bureau of Shipping of the League of Nations."

"That's a queer story!" growled the old sea captain, who was uncertain as to whether the announcement was a joke or not. "Do the passengers know about this?"

"No, Captain!"

"Good! This matter must remain a secret!" he commanded. "If that weary herd down there," he pointed to the promenade deck, "learns anything about this, they will storm the bridge out of curiosity. That's all!"

At the same instant, a wave of excitement ran through the crowd assembled at the railing. Voices were raised, and the people ran back and forth in such a manner that the planks creaked.

"An accident! An explosion!"

Arms pointed skyward.

A white cloud suddenly freed itself from the dark speck.

"Incredible!" mused the captain. "It is they!" He thereupon gave an order to prepare the motorboats.

Soon afterward the dark speck which was considered by the passengers to be an airship in distress, disappeared on the horizon. The white cloud came slowly down and for a long time remained visible in the evening sky, until it, too, touched the surface of the water and disappeared.

Meantime the ship had stopped. Two motor-boats shot out in the direction of the accident, and disappeared in the waves, as the *Cleopatra* began to follow the fast little boats.

The captain and ship's officers found difficulty in escaping the continuous questioning of the passengers, eager for sensation. The sailors were truly glad when, in an hour, the boats regained the ship, where all attention was centered upon them.

Hans Hardt was the first to ascend the rope ladder. He climbed slowly and painfully, like an old man. Dr. Hardt followed; then Tommy; and finally Anderl. They all found the unaccustomed gravity oppressive.

On looking up, they saw the railing crowded with an endless row of human heads, inspecting with curious eyes the new arrivals.

Anderl's leather breeches attracted especial attention.

"They appear to be either Germans or Austrians," said a withered little old lady, who was well-traveled, to a stocky Yankee who was her neighbor. He volunteered no reply, but, as though seeing a ghost, he stared at Tommy Bighead, who was just appearing on the promenade deck and making his way through the crowd.

"Tommy! Tommy Bighead!" he cried. "Is it really you? Can it be possible?"

Tommy turned around, and he smiled weakly on recognizing in the man a friend from Detroit.

"Very well," he replied. "Will you bet that it is really I?"

"Where on earth did you come from?"

"Not on earth." Tommy pointed upward and smiled mysteriously. "From the moon!"

THE END

Otto Willi Gail

Otto Willi Gail (b. 1896 in Gunzenhausen, middle Franconia—d. 1956 in Munich) was a science journalist and writer.

He studied electro-technology and physics. Besides his work for newspapers and radio he wrote books popularizing physics, astronomy and space travel. Gail also wrote several science fiction novels. Since he was in constant contact with the space travel pioneers at that time, such as Max Valier and Hermann Oberth, his novels were characterized by a wealth of scientific and technical knowledge.

Some of his best-selling novels, such as *The Stone From the Moon* and *The Shot Into Infinity* (available in Apogee/Black Cat editions), were translated and published in the United States. These novels, along with the present volume, were all based upon—and unified by—a consistent background (indeed, the entirety of Chapter XXVIII is more or less a summary of the underlying theme and numerous plot elements of *The Stone From the Moon*). This background was in turn heavily inspired by the work of one of the great scientific cranks of the twentieth century: Hanns Hörbiger. Many of Gail's ideas—especially those regarding ancient world-wide catastrophes and the similarities between the folklore and myths of various cultures, presage the pseudoscientific work of Immanuel Velikovsky and Erich von Daniken.

For his inspiration about the details of his spaceship, Gail turned to another expert, albeit one somewhat saner and more knowledgeable than Hörbiger: Austrian rocketry pioneer Max Valier.

HÖRBIGER AND THE WORLD ICE THEORY

Welteislehre (also known as *Glazial-Kosmogonie*) was first published in 1913 by an Austrian refrigeration engineer named Hanns Hörbiger. The basis of the theory is that most objects in our solar system besides Earth and the Sun are made out of ice or are at least covered in an extremely thick layer of it.

Hörbiger is said to have developed his theory after observing the Moon at night. He concluded from the strong reflection of the light and the structure of the impact craters that the moon must be made of ice. He further theorized that the entire Milky Way must be a collection of nearby icy bodies rather than distant stars..

Hörbiger explained the origin of the universe as the collision of a glowing mass of gigantic proportions with a smaller mass of solid ice. This led to an enormous explosion and the creation of our solar system. Ever since, existence has been based on an eternal struggle between fire and ice. It is no accident that this has strong similarities with Norse mythology.

Another aspect of the Welteislehre was the thought that Earth attracted numerous smaller planetary bodies. A planet would be caught in by the Earth, gravitating around it for some time before eventually colliding. At that time, natural catastrophes would occur all over the world. In a recuperating period, the planet would exist without a moon until the next planet would be attracted. Hörbiger believed that the current version of the Moon was the sixth since the formation of Earth and that a future collision would be inevitable. Believers in Welteislehre argued that the great flood described in the bible and the destruction of Atlantis were caused by previous collisions. The system somewhat resembles the later cosmic catastrophism of Immanuel Velikovsky.

Hörbiger published his theory in 1913 in his book *Glazial-Kosmogonie*. He also provided numerous tables and graphs trying to prove his theory. Most of these however were lacking substance and Welteislehre was quickly disregarded in scientific circles. The fact that it showed several parallels to early Greek and Nordic mythology did not help his cause among scientists.

One of the early supporters of Hörbiger's theories was Houston Stewart Chamberlain, the leading theorist behind the early development of the National Socialist Party in Germany in 1923. Through Chamberlain's influence Welteislehre became official Nazi policy in cosmology. Although Hörbiger died in 1931, his theory gained new momentum in the Third Reich. Heinrich Himmler, one of the most powerful Nazi leaders, became a strong proponent of the theory and he stated that if it was corrected and adjusted with new scientific findings it could very well be accepted as scientific work. In 1942 Hitler reasoned that the cold years in the early 1940s led him to believe in the correctness of the Welteislehre.

It is said that the real reason both Hitler and Himmler referred to the theory was to counterbalance the Jewish influence on the sciences, similar to the Deutsche Physik movement. Hörbiger's theory particularly opposed the theory of relativity, developed by Albert Einstein. A growing group of 'believing scientists' expanded the theory during the last years of World War II. Dozens of scientific journals, books, and even novels were published on this topic. Hörbiger's theories became generally accepted among the population of Nazi Germany.

The theory was quickly discredited again after the war. Nevertheless public opinion shifted at a much lower pace. A survey conducted in 1953 showed that over a million people in Germany, England, and the U.S. believed that Hörbiger was correct.

MAX VALIER

Max Valier was an Austrian rocketry pioneer. He helped found the German Verein für Raumschiffahrt (VfR or "Spaceflight Society") that would bring together many of the minds that would later make spaceflight a reality in the twentieth century.

Valier was born in Bozen (now Bolzano, Italy) in the South Tyrol and studied physics at the University of Innsbruck. He also trained as a machinist at a nearby factory. His studies were interrupted by the First World War, during which he served in the Austro-Hungarian army's air corps as an aerial observer.

After the war, Valier did not return to his studies, but became a freelance science writer. In 1923, he read Hermann Oberth's landmark book *Die Rakete zu den Planetenräumen* (The Rocket into Interplanetary Space) and was inspired to write a similar work to explain Oberth's ideas in terms that could be understood by a lay person. With Oberth's assistance, he published *Der Vorstoß in den Weltenraum* (The Advance into Space) the following year. It was an outstanding success, selling six editions before 1930. He followed this with numerous articles on the subject of space travel, with titles like "Berlin to New York in One Hour" and even a science fiction story, "A Daring Trip to Mars". His articles, accompanied by the remarkable illustrations of the Römer brothers, were published widely throughout Europe and in translation in England and the United States.

He actively publicized his incremental scheme for the development of a spaceship. He proposed the idea that a spaceship could be gradually evolved from a conventional aircraft. In doing so, he frequently enlisted the services and designs of such well-known aircraft designers and builders as Hugo Junkers and Alexander Lippisch, modifying them according to his own ideas.

Once model rocket-propelled airplanes had been successfully tested, full-scale rocket engines would be installed in the all-metal tri-motor Junkers G-24 transport aircraft, behind the two external, wing-mounted piston engines. The basic rocket airplane (Type 1) would take off using its conventional piston engines, not switching them off and converting to rocket power until a safe altitude has been reached.

Once this had been proven successful the next transition type would be built: a rocket-plane with an auxiliary piston engine (the middle engine of the three motors being retained). Four rocket engines would be installed in the wings and the wingspan shortened. This would be the Type 2, based upon the Junkers G-31, because its elevated tail unit would be more effective in avoiding the rocket's exhaust. Valier believed that this machine could cover distances of up to 2,000 km at altitudes of 50 km in 30 minutes. If two refueling stations were to be provided in the Atlantic, it could fly from Berlin to New York in three hours (two hours of actual flying time).

When enough flight experience had been gained, a pure rocket-plane would be flown. Six engines would be installed in the wings, which would have been shortened even further. The auxiliary piston engine would be eliminated. This design, Type 3, developed in 1927, had a pressurized cabin and a spindle-shaped, streamlined fuselage. The wings were equipped with slats and landing flaps. Direct intercontinental stratosphere flights could be made with this machine, Valier believed..

The penultimate step is the rocket ship, also developed in 1927. It would be a wingless, finned torpedo carrying fourteen rocket engines. These would be mounted in streamlined outrigger pods, seven motors to each. Seventy-five percent of its launching weight would be fuel. The rocket would be held in a vertical position for takeoff by a launching tower. It would attain an altitude of 250 km in five minutes.

When challenged that no pilot would ever be foolhardy enough to fly in one of these rockets, Valier replied, "...in the war, I was detailed to the testing of new aircraft types more than once. Of course, one prefers to climb into an old tested machine rather than into a new one, in which one cannot tell whether the innovations will stand the test. But after all an operational sortie was no life insurance either, and in spite of this enough volunteers signed on in the air force.—I shall, of course, be a member of the first crew that flies a rocket-plane."

The final objective of Valier's evolutionary scheme of development was the space ship: a design based partly on concepts invented by Hermann Oberth. Two ellipsoidal passenger compartments would be contained in the nose. The bulk of the rocket was occupied by tanks of fuel, in the midst of which—at the rocket's center of gravity—were gyroscopes. Eight large rocket engines surrounded the tail assembly, roughly amidship.

Max Valier's
Incremental Spaceship Design

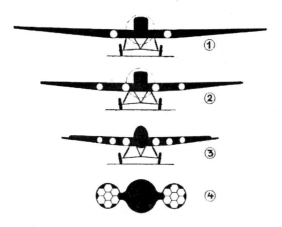

① ② ③ ④

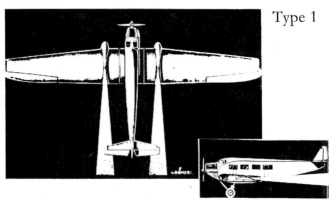

Type 1

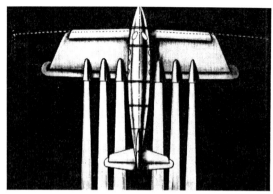

Type 3

Dotted lines indicate
width of the wings
of Type 2.

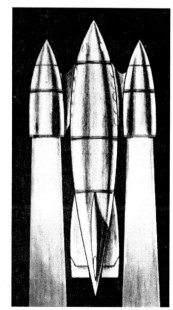

Type 4

• Otto Willi Gail

Also in 1927, Valier proposed two additional designs for long-range rocket aircraft. One was an enormous aircraft with a twin fuselage and twenty rockets mounted in the trailing edge of the vast wing and ignited in pairs. The passengers would be carried in the thick leading edge. The transoceanic rocket plane would cover the distance from Berlin to New York in 93 minutes.

Valier also designed a rocket-propelled sport airplane in 1927 (Type 6). It was a sleek-looking high-wing, open cockpit monoplane, not dissimilar to the Curtiss "Junior," with a streamlined fuselage, twin tail and a rocket engine mounted above the wing. At the front of the rocket module was a radial piston engine (though this would ultimately be done away with).

In 1928 and 1929 he worked with Fritz von Opel on a number of rocket-powered cars and aircraft. For von Opel, these were publicity stunts for the Opel company, for Valier they were a way of further raising interest in rocketry amongst the general population. By the late 1920s, the VfR was focusing its efforts on liquid-fuel rockets. Their first successful test firing with liquid fuel occurred in the Heylandt plant on January 25, 1930. On April 19, 1930, Valier performed the first test drive of a rocket car with liquid-fuel propulsion, the Valier-Heylandt Rak 7.

Valier was killed less than a month later when an alcohol-fueled rocket exploded on his test bench in Berlin.

Ron Miller